"How about we make a real date? For Friday," I suggested.

She was shaking her head. "No good. I've got to come over here every night to see how the workmen are doing, and the tension would be nearly unbearable." She was clearly joking now, confident.

"Okay," I stammered while my mind searched for a quick and witty solution. But I came up with nothing. Shrugging my shoulders, I lifted both hands in the air, palms upward. "Do you have any suggestions?"

Her brows pulled together and she frowned briefly before lifting her eyes back to mine. They were almost sultry.

"Why don't you just come over here and kiss me?"

Visit

Bella Books

at

BellaBooks.com

or call our toll-free number

1-800-729-4992

TREASURED PAST

BY
LINDA HILL

Bella
BOOKS

2004

Bella Books, Inc.
P.O. Box 10543
Tallahassee, FL 32302

First published 2000 by Naiad Press

Printed in the United States of America on acid-free paper
First Edition

Editor: Lila Empson
Cover designer: Bonnie Liss (Phoenix Graphics)

ISBN 1-59493-003-1

For my family—
Kate, Molly, and Maggie

Acknowledgments

Thanks to the members of my family, who continue to grow and scatter throughout the country. No matter how far away, they remain close in my heart.

Special thanks and much love to Barb and Ann, who have supported me in so many different ways over the years. Life is very full, indeed.

Chapter 1

I could feel the familiar rush of adrenaline curling up my spine as the auctioneer turned to his left.

"The next item up for bid." He paused as he peered over the glasses that slipped low on the bridge of his nose. He appeared to be having trouble focusing on the sheet of paper he held in one hand. "Item six-seventeen. Early American barrister bookcase by Stickley. Circa nineteen-twenty."

I tried not to smile and tip my hand. Not that anyone was paying attention, of course. I knew that. But it didn't matter. It was all part of the game.

"Shall we start the bidding at one hundred dollars?" He snapped the eyeglasses from his nose and scanned the crowd from right to left.

I waited impatiently, not taking a breath. It was part of my strategy. Be patient. Don't bid too quickly. Don't let the competition know that you're interested.

"One hundred dollars? Anyone?" He was frowning now.

Dammit. If I didn't bid now, he could pull it off the block. I raised my bid card, just enough so that he could see me.

"I have one hundred. Do I have one-fifty?" I didn't even have a chance to breathe before he was looking back at me. "I have one-fifty. Do I have two?"

Again the rush shot through me. The bidding was on. I set my jaw and raised my bid card.

"Two hundred. Do I have two-fifty?"

Back and forth. Back and forth. I could barely nod my head before he was looking at me again, waiting for my acceptance.

"Do I have five hundred?"

Dammit. I felt a frown pulling between my eyebrows. Who in the hell was bidding against me, anyway? I didn't want to go past six hundred dollars. It didn't matter that the bookcase was worth twice that amount. It was the principle. The real thrill came from picking something up for far less than it was worth. If I paid full price, somehow I never loved it once I got it home.

My nod was firm.

"Five hundred. Do I have five-fifty?"

I turned my head and followed his gaze, my eyes narrowing as I tried to find my competitor. My focus lapsed, and I almost laughed. I should have known. It was *her.* Not that I knew who *she* was. Only that I always seemed to run into her at these places and that we always seemed to be interested in the same items.

I watched her closely, willing her to look my way and take my challenge. She was raising a thin arm and nodding at the auctioneer.

"Do I have six hundred?"

Gritting my teeth, I raised my bid card without removing my gaze from the woman. She looked older than usual tonight, almost dowdy. Her dark hair was pulled tight behind her head and pinned up somehow. She wore a simple, short-sleeve blouse over a peasant skirt. Even from a distance, I could see her jaw working as she contemplated whether or not to raise the bid.

If she could read the thoughts that I was throwing her way, then she knew that I was daring her to do it. She knew that I would outbid her. I nearly always did.

In one motion, she made a curt nod toward the auctioneer before her eyes were on mine, her light gray eyes throwing the challenge back my way.

"Do I have seven hundred?"

Her face softened as we continued to stare. She looked tired. Dark circles lingered under those eyes.

"Six-fifty going once." I could hear the auctioneer's voice above the humming in my ears.

"Six-fifty going twice."

She was almost smiling. I was sure that I could see relief spreading over her and a smile creeping to her lips.

It's your last chance. Bid! Bid now!

I could hear my inner voice screaming, but I ignored it.

"Sold to bidder number two-seventeen." The sound of the gavel dropping shook me, and I glanced briefly in the direction of the noise. When I glanced back, the woman was no longer looking my way. Instead she was reviewing the list of items up for bid. I stared for a while, willing her to look my way, but got nothing in return.

I was disgusted with myself. How could I have let such a gorgeous piece like that go? And for what? I stared back at the woman again. It meant nothing to her. There was no excitement on her face, no thrill of victory. Not so much as a smile or a nod or a thank-you thrown my way.

My enthusiasm was gone. I said a few excuse-me's and made it to the nearest exit, dumping my bid card in the trash can as I passed.

Chapter 2

There were times when I wished that I'd never given up my own practice, and this was one of them. It was five-thirty on a Friday afternoon, and I should have been almost home by now, getting ready for the weekend. Instead, I was sitting behind my desk, fingers drumming on my desk pad, while I waited. And waited. I was supposed to be going to my parents' house for some sort of fund-raising dinner for their favorite charity of the month. If I didn't leave soon I wouldn't have time to go home and change.

And at this rate, I knew I wouldn't have time to pick up Beth.

At four-forty-five, Donald Gold had stuck his head in my office to tell me that he needed to speak with me before the day was over. In my mind, the day had been over half an hour ago. But Donald was a partner in the firm, and I knew I had no choice but to wait.

I rubbed one hand across my brow before I pushed myself away from the mahogany desk and practically leapt from the overstuffed leather chair. Everything about my office was lavish and over priced, from the furniture to the law books that lined each wall to the thick carpet that now muffled the sound of my footsteps as I approached the single vertical window that adorned one corner of the office.

From the thirty-seventh floor I had a bird's-eye view of the snarling traffic below. The expressway was a parking lot in both directions. The on-ramps to Storrow Drive and the Mass Pike were choked with merging vehicles.

Now I was frowning. I didn't have to deal with the downtown traffic when I'd had my own practice. My old office had been in a relatively quiet Cambridge neighborhood, just a few miles from my home in Newton.

Now I was laughing at myself. I may have been only a few blocks from home back then, but I never left the office until late in the evening. By contrast, in my new position with Brown, Benning, and Gold, I never hung around much after five o'clock. The differences in my life were measurable, in more ways than one.

"Sorry to keep you waiting." Donald's voice startled me. He was pulling out a chair from the round conference table and motioning me to join him. "This takeover business with McGrue and Son is coming to a boil." He rubbed tanned, speckled hands together as his eyes gleamed. "It won't be much longer now." I tried to ignore the glee in his voice. Tried not to think about how John McGrue would be feeling this weekend, knowing that the company he'd built for himself and his family for thirty years was about to be taken over by a large corporate giant.

Donald was patting the table. "Sit down. Join me."

I did as I was told, wishing fervently that I was outside in the traffic instead.

"You used to practice family law. Is that right?"

I nodded. "Twelve years."

I was expecting him to tell me that I should go back to family law. That I was a lousy litigator and that it was clear that I didn't give a hoot about the corporate clients that lined the pockets of our firm. I was wrong.

"You handled divorce cases?"

My internal warning lights were flashing. I nodded slowly.

"Good." Donald wasted no time. "I want you to represent my son in his divorce." He folded his hands together.

"With all due respect, sir —" He raised his hand in a no-argument salute.

"This isn't an option, Kate." He dropped his voice down and leaned forward, voice full of gravity. "I expect that the divorce might get a bit sticky, and I need this handled by someone internally. Someone that has my best interest at heart." He was staring into my eyes, not dropping his gaze.

"With all due respect, sir" — I cleared my

throat — "I was never a particularly good divorce attorney."

"Of course you were." His grin had a hint of evil. "You just usually found yourself representing the wrong client."

I could feel my face grow hot. In the majority of the divorce cases I'd handled in the past, my clients were lesbians who had found themselves in the unfortunate state of holy matrimony. The fact that nearly all of their husbands were bitter, resentful, and in denial about their soon-to-be ex-wives made my job difficult and painful.

I didn't know how to answer him. So I stared back into his tired green eyes and tried not to notice the wrinkles that so deeply lined his face. It was a face aged by too much tanning and too much drinking, I imagined. Silver hair combed perfectly to tame what had once been a curly mass. The white shirt that he wore was so tight and held so much starch that his neck bulged above the neckline.

He tapped a single finger on the tabletop, and my eyes dropped quickly, taking in the stiff white cuffs that contrasted so much with his tanned skin. He wore two rings. On his right hand he wore a thick gold band that held a single large ruby. On the other, he wore the class ring from Harvard Law School, 1944.

He was waiting for my response, but I wouldn't give him one. My ignoring his insult was the right approach, and I felt a small sense of triumph when he fidgeted nervously.

"In any case" — he cleared his throat — "my son needs a good divorce attorney, and so the case is yours." He unfolded his bulk from the chair and drew

8

toward the door. "I'll go over the details with you next week. I want this handled as quickly and quietly as possible."

My teeth were grinding as I watched him reach for the door.

"What exactly might get sticky about this case, Donald?" My voice sounded petulant. I could only image what kind of trouble Donald Junior could have gotten himself into.

Donald Gold turned back to face me, eyebrows pulled together as he stood tall. "His wife had an affair with another woman," he stated flatly. Only his slightly raised eyebrow let me know that he was mocking me.

"Bastard." I was still fuming when I came to a screeching halt near the end of my parents' driveway. Cars were everywhere, parked along the horseshoe drive beyond the gates and flowing out to the street below. Without hesitating, I shifted gears and pulled into the driveway, whipping past the parked vehicles and reaching for the garage opener. There was always an extra space for me inside.

I sneaked a quick peek at myself in the rearview mirror and grimaced. Mascara had settled in creases beneath blue eyes, and a light sheen had settled on my brow. Pulling a tissue from the glove compartment, I wiped it over my face and didn't bother with another inspection before stepping out of the car.

The kitchen door was slightly ajar and I sneaked in, finding myself in the middle of a circus of servers juggling trays of appetizers and drinks as they made their way in and out of the kitchen. My eyes searched for Maria's familiar face but came up empty. It wasn't a good sign if Maria wasn't in there. She ruled the kitchen with an iron fist, and she didn't like anyone, especially hired caterers, messing up her space.

Mindful of the servers around me, I waited until one of them looked like he was making an exit through the swinging doors to the dining room before I stepped up behind him, following him through the door.

I knew immediately why Maria was out here instead of in the kitchen. The sheer volume of people was so unexpected that I took a step back. What were my parents thinking? There had to be hundreds. And no doubt Maria was among them somewhere, making sure that everyone had plenty of food and drink.

"There you are, darling." My mother linked an arm through mine as she kissed my cheek. "I think your father's gone mad. Just look at this crowd." She was shaking her head, but the smile on her face gave her away. She was never angry with my father.

"How many people are here?" I asked, stepping out of the line of fire of the kitchen door and pulling her with me.

She shrugged. "Too many." She laughed as she hugged my arm closer. She was wearing a simple, off-white dress that fit her small frame snugly. Her blond hair had been cut shorter than I'd seen in a long time, a blunt cut several inches above her shoulder.

"You cut your hair."

She turned to smile at me, blue eyes sparkling. "I thought it was about time."

Mom had always had long hair, from as long ago

as I could remember. More often than not she'd pulled it back and away from her face, but every now and then she'd let it go free.

"I'm getting too old for long hair."

"Don't say that, Mom. You're not old." But even as I denied it, I could see the growing lines on her face. I did a quick calculation. She was fifty-eight. Twenty years older than myself. But she was in remarkable shape. I envied her thick, blond hair and trim figure. Unfortunately, the only thing I'd inherited from my mother's side was her blue eyes. The rest of my body came directly from my father's genes. I blamed my dark brown wavy hair, wide nose, and stocky body all on my dad.

"Will Beth be joining us this evening?" In spite of the crowd around us, my mom was completely focused on me. I loved the skill she had of making everyone she laid eyes on feel special.

"She said that she'd meet me here. And she's just a friend, Mom," I groaned, and watched her laugh.

"I can always hope, dear," she whispered, giving my arm another squeeze. My parents were hippies from long before I was born. Liberal to their very core, and I loved them for it. They were also ridiculously wealthy, another thing I hadn't minded in my youth.

Maria approached us, eyes in a fury as she barely acknowledged me before turning to my mother. She was speaking so fast that I barely understood her, her accent more pronounced than ever. My mother's attention shifted smoothly, focusing on calming Maria's temper.

As I let my eyes scan the room, it took a few moments for me to notice all the pieces of furniture that just didn't belong. Antique desks, tables, and cabinets were strewn throughout the dining and living rooms, sprinkled between various works of art. At least I assumed it was art, since I didn't have the best eye for these things. But the antiques — the roll-top desk and mission chair — now those I recognized and knew. My heart rate picked up a notch.

"Mom! What *is* all this stuff?"

Placated, Maria kissed me on the cheek to welcome me properly before disappearing into the kitchen.

"I'm sure I told you, dear."

"I probably wasn't listening."

She laughed. "It's an auction. Your father's had everyone he knows donate all kinds of art and collectibles that we're going to auction off tonight. All of the money is going to the New England Animal Shelter."

I couldn't control the way my eyes jumped from one piece to another. "Mom, you know this is my weakness. I would have remembered if you'd said there would be antiques."

"Don't worry, Katie. You don't have to bid on anything."

I was aghast. "Are you crazy? Of course I want to bid. But I didn't bring my checkbook."

My mother was laughing at me now. "Your credit is good with us, honey. You can send a check tomorrow." She gave me a little nudge. "Go on and take a look around. You haven't got much time. I think they're going to start bidding in about twenty minutes."

She didn't have to give me any more encouragement. The pressure of time enveloped me, and I felt anxiety rising. Not much time for an adequate appraisal. Without dawdling, I quickly stepped away and bypassed the mission rocker to approach the roll-top desk.

My first motion was to reach out and run a finger along the curved surface of the roll-top, tucking a finger into the small notch handle and lifting it open. It rolled smoothly, and I was instantly enamored. I had been collecting mahogany pieces for years, but was finding my taste running to oak these days. The gleaming oak beneath my fingertips spoke to me as I pulled open one drawer after another, checking for the smoothness of the pulls and fingering all the nooks and crannies.

My mind made up, I moved on. I spared only a glance at the school desk with the built-in inkwell. The collection of crockery didn't hold my interest, and neither did the deco end tables.

The next piece grabbed my attention. It was a large oak barrister bookcase, not unlike the one that I had bid on and lost just a week before. I counted the five pocket shelves and reached out to lift one door, quickly satisfied when it glided open smoothly. If I had been excited over the desk, now I was ecstatic. After testing each door separately, I stepped back to admire the piece, barely believing my luck. It was at least as nice as the one I'd lost the other night. Maybe even nicer. Hell, it could be the *same* piece for all I knew.

"Look familiar?" The woman's voice was nearly a whisper in my left ear. Startled, I turned abruptly. It took a moment before the image registered. I knew this woman. We'd never actually met, but I knew her.

Her face was just inches from mine, and I realized that we'd never been so close. Her face was rounder than I imagined, her eyes a startling shade of gray.

The hair that always seemed beyond control was smoothed back into a single knotted braid. She didn't look as old as I'd thought, either, although there were a few creases around her eyes.

It took far too long for me to digest her words and the situation.

Finally I reacted. "Is this the same one?"

She seemed amused by my stammering as she nodded. "It certainly is." Her words were like a sigh as she turned her eyes to the bookcase. "This one's a little tough to part with," she admitted.

"I can't believe you're letting it go. Especially to charity!" I remembered the way I'd driven up the bidding and felt a wave of guilt. "If I had known you were going to give it away I never would have bid so high on it," I told her.

An ironic smile lighted her features. "I hadn't known I was going to give it away at the time. But Jonathan can be quite persuasive."

"He certainly can be," I agreed without bothering to mention that Jonathan was my father.

"So are you going to bid on it tonight?" she asked.

"I have to! I can't let it get away from me twice in one week!" I laughed, and was rewarded with a broad smile. She had always looked so serious when we were bidding against each other. I don't believe I'd ever seen her smile. But then again, I imagined that I must look pretty fierce myself when in a serious bidding battle.

"What about you?" I asked. "Do you see anything here that you're interested in?"

She wrinkled her nose and glanced around. When I

saw her looking in the direction of the desk, I nearly jumped out of my skin. "Please don't say you're interested in the desk. I wouldn't want to bid against you tonight."

Now she laughed. "No, no. I'm afraid it's too pricey for me. Unless of course the bidding doesn't go too high . . ." It took me a moment to realize that she was teasing me, and I felt a smile on my lips. She was much more attractive and enjoyable than I'd imagined.

"Well, well. Two of my very favorite women." My father curled his arms around our waists, and I felt myself begin to bristle. How in hell did he know this woman so well?

He bestowed his most winning smile on the woman beside me before dropping a kiss on my cheek. "I'm so glad you could make it, honey."

"Hi, Dad." I gave him a quick hug and didn't miss the way *she* raised both eyebrows as she mouthed the word *Dad*. I decided to ignore her.

"Sorry I'm so late. One of the partners kept me for a meeting that I couldn't get out of," I explained quickly.

"My daughter the lawyer," he teased. One of his favorite pastimes was teasing me about how I'd sold out to the corporate world.

"Well, that explains it." The unnamed woman found her voice.

I looked at her, unable to read the tone in her voice. "Explains what?"

"The suit." She nodded back at me, and I glanced down, taking in the perfect navy suit and starched white shirt. I found myself feeling defensive.

15

"I've only seen you in jeans," she explained.

My dad glanced quickly between us. "You two *do* know each other, don't you?"

I smiled and she laughed. "Not really," I began, while she tried to explain.

"We've bumped into each other at several auctions, actually. But we've never been introduced."

"Then forgive me my poor manners," my father said smoothly. "Annie, this is my very favorite daughter, Katherine Brennan." He dropped his voice conspiratorially. "Of course she is my *only* daughter and a lawyer at that, but we've forgiven her."

Annie smiled and laughed in all the right places.

My father turned to me. "And this, my dear, is Annie Walsh. Annie owns an absolutely exquisite shop in Cambridge called Treasured Past. She also does quite a bit of charity work with your mother and me." He was beaming as he glanced between us.

"A pleasure." Annie was smiling as she held out her hand. At least I thought it was a smile. But something inside said it was closer to a smirk.

"My friends call me Kate," I replied as I took her hand in mine. Her grip was firm, hands rough. I glanced down. Working hands.

My father was checking his watch. "I have to run. The bidding should be starting any minute now, and I have to kick off the show. Are you going to be around this weekend?" He directed the question to me.

"It depends. If I get lucky tonight, I may have to come back tomorrow with the truck." I remembered the roll-top desk.

"So you'll be bidding?" he smiled.

"Is there any doubt?" I asked, and he laughed.

"Good." He began to step away. "Spend some of

that money, will you? The shelter could use it." He turned and disappeared in the crowd while Annie and I stood awkwardly looking, but not looking, at each other.

Chapter 3

I spent the next day loading and unloading both the bookcase and the desk, grumbling the entire time that I'd paid too much for each of them. For the life of me, I couldn't figure out what had come over me. I was as fierce as ever, raising the bid to outrageous amounts without blinking an eye. I had been determined that the antiques would be mine, regardless of the cost.

"What was I thinking?" I grumbled.

"Are you sure you weren't just trying to impress her?"

I threw a withering glance in Beth's direction. "Impress who?" I asked, knowing perfectly well whom she was referring to.

"Annie. Your nemesis."

"Pfft. Annie." I said her name aloud for the first time.

"You were much cozier with her than I was." I nearly dropped my end of the desk, and decided it was time to take a break. Beth followed suit, gently placing two legs on the carpet.

Beth was grinning as she came to stand beside me and leaned against the desk. "We were talking about you the entire time. We couldn't believe the way you were bidding. Like a maniac."

"Ha." I stepped away and disappeared into the kitchen, grabbing two colas from the refrigerator before returning. "And every time I heard you two snickering over there I was more determined than ever to bid even higher."

"I know. It was hysterical."

"Very funny." I handed one of the sodas to her and watched her open it. Beth had thick, short blond hair, blue eyes, and was slender as a stick. But she was stronger than I was, and far more feminine. I had known her for countless years, and she was my dearest friend.

"It *was*. You should have seen the way your jaw was set. As soon as Annie saw it she nudged me and said, 'Watch, here we go.'"

"Very funny," I repeated, and snapped back the tab of my drink. "What was I thinking? I spent almost twenty-five hundred dollars." I took a long drink.

"I know," Beth laughed. "I saw you. But at least it was for charity."

"That's what I keep telling myself. Charity." I glanced at the desk and then down the hall. "Where am I going to put this thing?"

Beth shrugged. "Get rid of the one you have now. You've been complaining about it for at least a year."

I thought about it for a moment. "I know, but it's mahogany. Everything I have in the study is mahogany. The roll-top won't match."

Beth shrugged again. "You've been leaning toward the oak for a while now. Maybe it's time to replace everything." She took another sip of soda.

The idea appealed to me. And I was more than halfway there now that I owned both the oak desk and bookcase. But the thought of trying to unload the old stuff made me cringe.

"How would I get rid of the old stuff? The last thing I want to think about is trying to sell it."

Beth's eyes twinkled. "Maybe Annie would be willing to take it on in her store. You should give her a call."

Annie. The name rolled so smoothly from her lips, the name already a part of our lives.

"Sure," I said. "I can see the smirk on her face now."

Beth laughed. "We were just *teasing* you, Kate. We were having fun. You should call her. Maybe she can help."

I contemplated it for a moment, running through the idea in my mind. I could wander into her shop and see what it was like. I'd have an excuse . . .

I didn't like the direction of my thoughts.

"You like her, don't you?" Beth's words startled me.

"Please. I don't know her."

"Of course you do. You've been talking about her ever since that auction back in Springfield."

"Yeah, about how pissed I was every time I ran into her and she bid against me." I crossed my arms. "You know, I never even thought that she might have a shop. I always assumed she was just this eccentric woman who had the same taste in antiques that I did."

"Eccentric how?" Beth's eyebrows pulled together.

I shrugged and thought about it for a moment. "I guess it was the way she was usually dressed. Peasant dresses and big skirts, with her hair all messed up."

Beth wrinkled her nose. "She certainly didn't appear that way last night. I thought she looked almost" — Beth tilted her head as she tried to come up with the right word — "cultured. And she was very nice."

My laugh was sarcastic. *"Nice?* The woman is a shark."

"Oh, and you're not?"

"You got there late. You don't know her." I was becoming unreasonable.

"And you do?"

"No," I admitted.

Silence stretched between us.

"But you'd like to?" Beth's voice was quiet.

"Beth!"

"I wouldn't blame you, Kate. She's a very attractive woman."

"You're forgetting at least one minor detail," I told her. "She's probably straight."

Beth grimaced. "You have a point there, sweetie.

But you never know. She seemed at least very woman-identified. I don't think I saw her talk to a single man last night. Except for your father, of course."

Thinking of my father made me laugh. "You thought *I* was wild last night. He was an animal."

"He was, wasn't he?" Practically a part of our family, Beth was especially fond of my dad. "I don't think I've ever seen him so wound up. They must have pulled in a fortune!"

"Twenty-five grand," I told her.

She let out a low whistle. "Wow. Over a hundred people there, and you manage to contribute exactly ten percent to the cause," she teased. "Yikes."

"It was for charity."

"Uh-huh. And to impress Annie."

There it was. That name again. "Why does the conversation keep going back to her?"

"Because I know you, Kate. Call her."

I rolled my eyes, feigning exasperation, but knew that Beth wasn't buying it for a moment.

"All right." I caved in. "I'll drop by her shop."

Beth didn't bother trying to hide her grin.

Chapter 4

Donald was being an absolute prick. No matter how tactfully I tried to squirm out of representing his son in his divorce case, Donald wouldn't hear of it. He didn't exactly threaten me with my job, but I knew that making this case an issue would be the end of my career at Brown, Benning, and Gold.

I wasn't certain how I would feel if Donald decided to make my life hell and I was forced to leave the firm. The truth was that it was a job and nothing more, so I didn't think I would care much if I had to look elsewhere.

I'd found that corporate law was quite different from family law. To be a successful corporate attorney, you had to possess a cold heart and a spotless reputation. So far my reputation was clean enough, and my heart wasn't invested in the pockets of our business clients.

Not like my old practice. I'd cared far too much then.

When I lost a case, it was too close to home. The final straw had been a custody case. Beth had come to me, pleading for me to represent her in the custody hearing of her eight-year-old son. At the time, it didn't appear that her ex-husband was going to fight the custody. But that was before the hearing, and before he'd found out that his wife of ten years had decided that she was a lesbian.

Losing Beth's battle in the courtroom had devastated me. It had also been my last case. I cleaned out my office, gave notice to my landlord, and didn't go near a courtroom for nearly a year.

Becoming a ruthless corporate attorney had saved me, I reminded myself. "It sure beats the alternative," I muttered out loud.

"Okay, Donny Junior," I began, picking up the thin brown file that Donald had dropped off that morning. "Let's see if we can't make your daddy happy."

I walked past the antique store three times while I tried to gather the courage to step inside.

This is ridiculous, I told myself. *I have a legitimate reason to be here.*

I caught my reflection in the large display window

and realized that if anyone were watching, I must look like a complete fool. I decided to try to appear nonchalant, and slowly slipped my sunglasses to the end of my nose while I pretended to be fascinated by a Mickey Mouse watch that winked up at me from its original metal Fossil case. I knew that Mickey was popular, but I'd had no idea that his memorabilia was so valuable.

I stole a glance inside the store but could see no one milling about. I wasn't sure if this was good or bad. If someone else was there, I could pretend to browse awhile and get my thoughts in order and observe her from a distance. If not, I'd be forced to talk to her right away.

A sharp tap on the window snapped me to attention. *Christ.* The hand that was tapping on the window from inside the store belonged to none other than Annie Walsh. *Christ.* My heart slipped to my stomach when I recognized the grin on her face. Or perhaps I should have called it a smirk. That would have been closer to the truth, I think. Specifically, it was a rather self-satisfied I-told-you-so smile.

I knew that my own smile faltered as I returned the sunglasses to their rightful perch and waved halfheartedly. No turning back now.

I smoothed my already smoothed skirt as I turned on one heel and stepped to the door. She was on the other side when the small brass bell rang, announcing my arrival.

"Hi." My voice was breezy.

"Hi," she replied, the single syllable matching her raised brow. "Just passing by?" she asked, mocking me.

"No." I was irritated by her tone, which was of

course ridiculous, but I hated that I'd been bagged. "Actually, I came to talk to you."

She seemed surprised that I was so straight-forward, and stepped aside to welcome me into her shop. I took the moment to remove the sunglasses from my nose and take a quick glance around the store. I wasn't sure what I had expected. Lots of quaint antique furniture and knickknacks, I suppose. So I was surprised by the variety of objects and colors that lined every inch of the store.

"Wow." The word came out slowly, completely sincere. "This is nice." My eyes wandered from one display to the next. "I didn't expect that I'd want to shop, but I think I may have to browse around."

"I'm glad you like it." Her smile was finally sincere. I noticed that she was wearing a pair of jeans today, a departure from the skirts she normally wore. The long brown hair was as unruly as ever in its bundled-up state atop her head. She certainly was curious. "You've never been here before?"

"No." I shook my head. "I don't usually go to many antique stores, although I'm not quite sure why."

"Perhaps stores lack that certain thrill of anticipation and triumph that you get at an auction."

I stared at her dead-on. She was probably right, although I'd never given it a second thought before this moment.

"Maybe." I'd only give her that much. "I'm afraid I'm just not a very good shopper. Of anything, actually. I hate shopping."

She was holding back a smile, and it made me crazy. Was hating to shop a crime, for godsake? Un-American?

"I understand," she finally said. "I'm not a nut about shopping either, but I do like antiquing, in any form." She laughed, and I was charmed all over again. "Nothing's better than when you find a particular piece that you've been searching for forever. Unless of course it's in mint condition and the seller is asking far less than what it's worth. I admit I get an awful thrill out of that."

"A bigger thrill than outbidding me at auction?" I decided to try my hand at a bit of humor, and was rewarded with a sudden smile, followed by a grimace.

"The truth is that I always seem to bid too high when it's you I'm bidding against."

It was my turn to laugh. "I do too!"

"Now why do you suppose that is," she asked, and I could feel heat rising in my cheeks as our gazes locked. I couldn't stand it.

"It couldn't possibly have anything to do with my competitive nature, I'm sure," I told her.

"Nor my desire to win at all costs," she replied.

Again we laughed, eyes locking. Her gray eyes seemed to grow darker. This time I wasn't able to come up with a quick reply.

The silence stretched a little long, until she finally found the words to thankfully interrupt what I was certain was a longing look on my part.

"So what did you want to see me about?" She dropped her glance and stepped away from me, turning the corner until she was firmly planted on the other side of a long wooden countertop. I was thankful for the distance, and the distraction.

"I'm a bit embarrassed to tell you, so I'll come right out with it. You remember the desk and bookcase that I picked up the other night at the auction?"

Again that slow smile. "As if I could forget. You were in rare form that night."

I tried not to let her teasing get to me. "I know. I went a bit over the top."

"But you won," she interjected.

"Yes I did, and it was for charity," I reminded her.

"Uh-huh." I could barely tolerate her making fun of me, but I was determined not to let her get to me.

"Anyway . . ." I narrowed my gaze. "Once I brought it all home I realized that none of it goes with the furniture that I currently have in my office."

Her mouth flew open, her eyes horrified. "You're not going to give them up, are you?"

"No," I insisted. "I love those pieces and intend to enjoy them for a very long time. But the problem is that I have some mahogany pieces — desk, bookcase, and credenza — that I don't need any longer. I was wondering if you might take things on here for people, on consignment. Or if you might be interested in taking them off my hands."

The look on her face was difficult to interpret.

"So you're here on business."

I nearly choked while trying to figure out exactly what she meant by that. Was she disappointed?

"More or less."

She stared at me, and I watched the smile return.

"Actually," I stuttered, "Beth suggested that I call you to see if you'd be interested or if we could work out an arrangement. I didn't think you would, but thought I'd take a chance and drop in."

She smiled slowly, warming my innards. "Beth is very sweet. Have you known her long?"

The way she smiled when she mentioned Beth's name made me pause. It would be just my luck to find out that she was interested in Beth. *Get a grip*, I told myself. *You don't even know if she's a lesbian.*

"Many years," I replied, my voice steady. "Since high school."

Both eyebrows shot up. "Wow. That's a long time."

I grinned. "Are you insinuating that I'm an old woman?"

"God no." She laughed. "I'm sure I've got at least ten years on you."

I wanted to ask her age, but didn't.

"In any case, it sounds like I should probably take a look at this furniture of yours. I don't suppose you have a photo with you?"

I smiled sheepishly. I hadn't even thought to take one.

She shrugged. "That's okay. Perhaps I could come by and take a look?"

I stared at her, and blinked hard. I hadn't been prepared for this turn of events.

"Sure. That would be great," I finally spoke. "When's good for you?"

"Ah." She turned to pick up an appointment book and began flipping pages.

"Unfortunately, I'm only free on evenings and weekends," I told her.

"That's okay," she told me, glancing up. "What about Friday or Saturday evening? I close up shop around five o'clock."

My heart did an unexpected flip-flop. This felt too much like we were making a date.

"Friday's fine. I could even make dinner if you like." I nearly cringed as I said the words. *What was I thinking?*

"You cook?" She grinned.

I blanched. "Not really. But I do have a couple of dishes that I keep for occasions when it's absolutely necessary."

She laughed again, causing a tingle to flutter up my spine.

"Dinner on Friday it is, then. I can be there by six."

"Great. Let me give you my address."

I gave her directions to my house and watched her scribble down everything I said. I heard the tinkle of the bell above the door, and we both turned to see an older gentleman enter the store.

Annie greeted him and excused herself when he asked about a particular type of porcelain dish he was searching for. I didn't want to leave without saying good-bye, so instead I took the opportunity to browse around.

It didn't take me long to decide that I had been limiting myself all these years. Until now, my interest had always been exclusively in antique furniture. I'd been under the misconception that auctions were the best way to find good deals, but I soon realized that I'd been mistaken.

Not only did I find several pieces priced significantly cheaper than I'd expected, but I also found all kinds of treasures that set my adrenaline pumping. Clearly, I'd been missing out on quite a bit.

The first thing that attracted my was the rather large display of Coca-Cola items. There were advertising signs, a large neon clock bearing the Coca-Cola logo, napkin holders, and nearly anything else that I could imagine. But the item that really sent my blood pumping was the full-size Coca-Cola vending machine. It was the kind that I remembered from my childhood, that had a narrow glass door down the left side. Behind the door were round holes that held ten-ounce bottles of soft drink. The price of the soda was ten cents. I laughed and smiled all at once, memories flooding me.

I reached out and turned over the price tag, cringing as I let it fall back in place. Thirty-eight hundred dollars. *Yikes*.

"Pretty, isn't it?" I hadn't heard Annie sneak up on me.

"It's beautiful. Pricey, too. Is this a rare item?"

Annie's head dipped back and forth. "Yes and no. The old vending machines are somewhat rare. But the Coke ones are the easiest to find. This one's been completely restored. There's a guy down on the Cape that does a lot of work for me on some things that I find."

I nodded, standing quietly while I admired the machine. "Do you ever see a 7UP machine? Or Pepsi?"

Her eyes lit up. "Much harder to find. And double the price tag, easily."

I shook my head, admittedly feeling greedy. I suddenly wanted one, and had to laugh.

"I had no idea you could find stuff like this anymore," I muttered. "I'm afraid I've led a sheltered life."

Her raised brow told me that she didn't believe a word of it.

"No, no. I mean that for so many years I barely set foot outside of my office. I was never home, and I never even bothered to buy real furniture until about a year ago. My house is practically empty."

She looked at me oddly, and I realized I wasn't making any sense. "A year ago I realized that I was completely burned out and quit my job at the time. It wasn't until then that I started noticing things like this, and the oak office furniture. Does that make sense?"

"Sure, I suppose."

"I'm finding so many things that are new to me. I started out with a few pieces here and there. Mostly functional things like furniture and bookshelves. But looking around your shop, I can see that there's a whole other world of antiques and collectibles that I didn't even know about."

My eyes flitted across the narrow room, taking it all in. They focused on an old brass candlestick phone, and I heard myself gasp. "My god, is that real?" I turned and covered the eight steps between Annie and the tall display case behind her.

She laughed when she saw me staring at the phone, just inches from my face now. "It better be. I paid enough for it."

"Does it work?" I let one index finger trail along the shaft.

"Yes it does, actually. All my phones do."

"All?" Curious, I let my eyes go back to hers.

Her grin was somewhat sheepish.

"You've discovered my real weakness. I collect phones. Every one ever made. They only make it to the shop if I already have one in my personal collection. And of course whenever I see one that's in better shape than the one I already own, I have to buy it." She seemed embarrassed now. "It really is my weakness."

I let my eyes wander over her face.

"I'm glad to know you have one."

She laughed. "Why?"

"Because until now I thought you were almost perfect." I said the words before I realized how they might sound, and saw the color rush to her face.

She ignored me. "This one is a Western Electric. All original parts. The patent on it was nineteen-twelve."

Trying to recover, I tried to pay attention to what she was telling me.

"It's gorgeous," I muttered, picking up the price tag and flipping it over. Three hundred dollars. I whistled low.

She laughed at me. "Only two-fifty for you."

I caught the small crinkles around her eyes and felt my heart sink.

"Deal." The word was out before I could take it back.

"What?"

"Sold. I'll take it."

She raised a brow, and I could almost read her thoughts. She was probably thinking that it must be nice to be the daughter of wealthy parents. I wanted to change my mind, but it was too late. I honestly didn't like to flaunt money. But I couldn't help thinking that it seemed every time I was around Annie I was spending ridiculous amounts of money. "Like I said," I hastened to explain, "I'm really just beginning to decorate my home, and it's actually kind of stark." It was true. My walls were bare and my shelves empty.

She was smiling again. "Then you should come shopping more often!"

"Maybe I will," I told her. "Now that I know what wonderful stuff you have here."

The bell above the doorway tinkled again, and we

both glanced up. A rather short, elderly woman entered the small store.

I glanced at my watch and cringed. I was going to be late for my first meeting with Donald Junior.

"Wow. I'm running late. Will you take a check?"

"Of course," Annie told me.

I reached into my bag and pulled out my checkbook and pen, scribbling madly.

"So Friday at six?" she asked quietly.

Suddenly nervous again, I almost tore the check as I ripped it from its pad. "Friday at six," I told her.

The woman who had just entered the store was clearing her throat.

"Let me wrap the phone up for you," Annie suggested as she glanced at the woman and smiled.

"No, no," I told her. "I need to run. Why don't you just bring it with you on Friday?"

She shrugged. "You trust me with it for that long?"

"I guess I'll have to." I glanced at the woman who tapped her heel impatiently. "I'll see you. Thanks for your help."

"Thank you. Enjoy your day."

I smiled a reply and waved as I walked back out into the sunlight.

Chapter 5

Donald Gold Junior was creepy. I couldn't think of a better word to describe him. He was dressed perfectly in a three-piece suit, the cuffs of his white shirt starched just as stiff as his father's. I suppose he was attractive enough, handsome in fact. Wavy dark hair and a chiseled jaw. Teeth perfectly white and even.

But he wouldn't look at me. Except for the first moment when we shook hands, he wouldn't let me see his eyes. They shifted nervously, just as his body seemed to bounce in his chair as I asked him questions.

"There's no chance of reconciliation?"

"Hardly." His voice was harsh.

"What assets do you own jointly?"

"The house." He frowned. "I want the house," he snapped. It was the third time he'd said those words. He began to fidget again as his impatience grew. "I thought my father already went over all of this with you."

I tried to remain calm. "He did show me a short list of assets. Are you aware of what's on the list?"

"Of course I am. I'm the one that wrote it."

I nodded, biting my tongue.

"I want the house and all of the furnishings."

I nodded again, trying to control the frown that pulled at my lips.

"I'm not sure whether or not your father explained to you that under Massachusetts law —"

"I don't care about the law. I have ammunition. If she fights me on the house, I'll ruin her. It's that simple."

My throat grew tight.

For the first time since the beginning of our meeting, he met my eyes. "Did my father tell you what she did?"

I chose my words carefully. "He mentioned that there was a woman involved."

"Involved? How about bare-ass-naked-in-our-bed involved," he spat.

I wanted to throttle him right there.

"I really don't need you to go into the details right now, Mr. Gold."

"I'll spill everything if this divorce gets in front of

a judge." He placed both hands palm down on the table between us before lifting and pointing a finger at my face. "You make sure that her lawyer understands that, okay?"

I held my breath and swallowed the anger that was beginning to choke me. "I think I have enough information for now, Mr. Gold. If I have any other questions I'll be sure to give you a call."

He nodded, eyes shifting again. "I want this over with as soon as possible."

"I'll do my best, Mr. Gold." I stood up, dismissing him. Decorum suggested that I hold out my hand, but I refused. The thought of touching him made my skin crawl. "You'll hear from me soon."

Eyes shifting, he nodded his head, apparently satisfied. I did something unprofessional and turned away, busying myself with a deposition and fingering through several files. I didn't look up again until I knew he was gone. And when I did, I found myself nearly choking on my anger.

The situation was impossible.

Chapter 6

I hadn't been kidding when I'd told Annie that I didn't cook very often. In fact, it had probably been an understatement. Maria had cooked nearly every meal I'd ever eaten until I was twenty-two years old. I had attended Wellesley College for my undergraduate degree, and living at home was just too convenient and easy for me to consider leaving. Not to mention the fact that between my parents and Maria, I had been spoiled rotten.

Maria was a wonderful cook, and I had spent

many hours in my youth atop a kitchen stool pulled up close to the counter while I watched her prepare our meals. I spent hours watching as she chopped, grated, mixed, and poured as she created delightful delicacies of every kind. Italian was my mother's favorite, and Maria was a master. I had studied the way she layered lasagna noodles over ricotta cheese and meat sauce, and then added another layer before draping on the mozzarella.

Now as I stood in my kitchen, I couldn't quite remember the order that the different ingredients went into the dish. I was tempted to call Maria but decided that the order of the layers probably didn't matter. The sauce tasted near perfect, and that was what really mattered. I tasted the sauce one last time before grinning and sliding the dish into the oven.

Annie arrived right on time. She carried a bottle of Merlot in one hand and my candlestick phone in the other. Her smile was genuine as we greeted each other and awkwardly shuffled the wine and phone from her hands to mine.

"I'm so excited about my new phone. You'll have to help me decide where to put it," I chatted nervously as I led her from the front hallway and into the living room. I placed the phone down on the coffee table and excused myself while I deposited the bottle of wine in the kitchen.

When I returned, she was standing near the middle of the room, hands clasped behind her back as she tilted her head toward the ceiling. I followed the direction of her gaze and watched as her eyes trailed over the carvings of the molding that edged the ceiling.

"Very nice design. Is it all original work?"

I really had no idea what she was talking about. "I guess so. It was all there when I bought the place, so I can't be certain." The house was an old Victorian, with vaulted ceilings and intricate molding. It had been part of what had attracted me originally.

"It's exquisite."

I don't think I'd actually ever heard anyone say the word *exquisite* before, and I smiled at the word, thinking it perfect from her lips.

"Exquisite?"

Her eyes met mine. "Yes. Incredible detail. Are you mocking me, or do you really not know what you have here?"

I wasn't quite sure how to interpret the question.

"No," I stammered. "I mean, it's lovely to me, which is why I bought the place. But beyond that, no, I don't know what you mean."

She glanced around the room once more, eyes narrowing before she brought them back to me. "If it's all original, then you have a small fortune here. It's remarkable work, really. You don't see it very often anymore. Many people gutted their Victorians back in the fifties and sixties. Stripped everything down and modernized the rooms." She stepped toward the glass pocket doors that separated the living room from what had probably once been a parlor or great room.

Placing her hands on each door, she slowly pushed them apart and watched them glide smoothly open before disappearing into the walls. She stood back and shook her head. "This is wonderful."

"Thank you," I told her, slightly embarrassed. I looked past her and the open doorway and into the great empty room before her. It was probably larger than many apartments, with oak flooring and tall, white walls. But it was completely empty of furnishings. I rarely went in that room. The truth was that I rarely went into any of the rooms besides the study and the bedroom.

I had purchased my home many years before, just out of college. At the time I had imagined filling the rooms with many grand things. But somehow my work had gotten in the way until my home was just a place to fall asleep at night.

Now Annie was glancing back over her shoulder, one eyebrow raised and a smile on her lips. "You weren't kidding when you said the place was empty, were you?"

I laughed, a bit embarrassed. "You didn't believe me? I told you, I'm just now getting around to decorating." I took a few steps to stand beside her and we stared into the empty room together. "Unfortunately, decorating is not one of my talents. I may have to hire someone."

"That would be a shame!"

I wrinkled my brow in reply.

"Decorating should be fun. Something passionate that you can get excited about. Envisioning what you want the room to look like and then creating it and watching it come to life." Her voice was full of enthusiasm.

I frowned. "I hate to dampen your spirits, but there's just one small problem."

"Don't say you don't have time."

I laughed. "No, it's not that."

"Or money." There was definitely sarcasm in her voice.

"Talent." I shrugged. "I have none. I have no concept of what looks good together. This place would be a complete disaster if I let myself decorate."

Annie threw me a look that said she didn't believe a word of what I was saying. She turned back to the living room and glanced about. I followed her gaze and took in the coffee table on the simple throw rug in the center of the room. An overstuffed sofa lined one wall. A mission rocker stood beneath a tall lamp. A variety of potted plants stood against the window that faced the front of the house.

Her eyes rested on mine, and I could tell that she was struggling with what to say. Then a broad smile broke onto her lips.

"You have a gorgeous home, Kate. But you're right. You're either a horrible decorator or you just moved in last week." If anyone else had said those words to me, I probably would have been angry. But hearing the teasing tone in Annie's voice made me laugh.

"See? I told you and you didn't believe me, did you?"

"No," she laughed again. "I thought you were pulling my leg. I thought for sure that you must have this gorgeous home that would be decorated right out of a magazine."

"Like my parents' house?" I raised a brow.

Her smile faltered a bit, and I could almost read her mind. It was something that I'd seen on her face before, and I thought it had something to do with my parents' wealth.

"Daddy's spoiled little girl?" The words came out before I could stop them.

She dropped her eyes for a brief moment, and I knew I was right. Her smile was contrite.

"I apologize. I guess I made some assumptions when I found out who your father was."

I couldn't describe the emotion I was feeling. I know I was angry, but not at Annie. I was used to being treated as different when people discovered who my parents were, but my parentage had opened many doors for me. Doors that I took for granted. There had been times, however, when I saw the resentment on someone's face. Or when a new friend began treating me as someone with money instead of someone with whom she shared a bond. I didn't want Annie to be one of those people.

Apparently I didn't respond quickly enough, because Annie was frowning.

"Really, Kate. I'm sorry."

I waved her off. "I'm used to it." I felt my back stiffen and I felt the need to explain to her. "It's true that I've never lacked for money," I began. "I had a wonderful childhood and never had to worry about a thing. I know that I've been very fortunate. But I don't apologize for that. I've worked very hard all of my adult life." My mouth clamped shut, and I felt close to tears. *What in hell is wrong with me?* "My grandfather left me a fifty-thousand-dollar trust fund. I used that as a down payment on the house. My parents paid for my education, but I haven't taken a dime from them since." My chin lifted defiantly. *Why did I feel such a need to defend myself?*

I couldn't read her thoughts. Her face softened as she stared at me, then hardened. Then a slow smile spread across her features.

"I underestimated you, Kate. I'm sorry." She took one step toward me, raising a hand and then dropping it. "I won't do it again."

Her eyes were earnest, and my defenses fell.

"Apology accepted," I grinned.

"Actually, I knew from the first time that you outbid me that you must be a very assertive and independent woman. I guess discovering that you're Jonathan Brennan's daughter threw me off a little."

My mood lightened. "Did I really outbid you the first time?"

"Absolutely." She nodded toward the corner of the room. "You stole that mission rocker right out from under me."

"Ha!" I mocked her. "I picked that chair up for a song. You didn't bid nearly enough."

Now she shook her head. "Ah, but you had the advantage, my dear. I have to be able to turn things around and make a profit. I don't stand a chance when you keep driving up the price." She was lifting one hand, tucking an imaginary strand of hair behind one ear.

My head tipped to one side as I thought about her words. "Wow. I never thought of it that way. It must make it difficult sometimes."

"I take my chances," she replied. "Is that dinner I smell?"

I smiled nervously and nodded. "It should be ready by now."

"Then I think it's about time you invited me to sit down to dinner. I'm looking forward to trying your specialty."

I motioned for her to follow me into the kitchen.

"You *do* have a table and chairs, don't you?" She moved quickly back to her mocking tone.

"No," I said seriously. "I thought we'd just curl up on the couch with paper plates." I watched with glee as she tried to cover the horror on her face.

"I'm just kidding," I laughed. "Follow me."

Chapter 7

The evening went much better than I could have
hoped for. Annie raved about my lasagna, and I did
my best to accept her compliments graciously.
Conversation came easily, and we managed to get
through the evening without competing on any topic.
Annie was a wonderful conversationalist, animated,
intelligent, and thoughtful as our dialogue moved from
antiques to politics to current events. About the only
topic that we didn't discuss was our personal lives. I
admit that I was comfortable with that, although
slightly surprised. Two people didn't usually spend an

entire evening together without eventually speaking or inquiring about something personal.

She agreed to take my old office furniture to her shop on consignment, and I was most grateful. After a quick phone call to Beth, we arranged to load Beth's truck and take it all over to Annie's next Saturday. I was suddenly looking eagerly forward to the weekend.

I was tapping my pencil. Not a good sign.

The divorce papers that I'd filed the day before were just too simple. I'd never had to do so little in the way of documentation in preparation for filing for a client.

Every time I read the document, I felt sure that something was missing. But for the life of me, I couldn't figure out what it might be.

It troubled me that a forty-eight-year-old man, whose father was extremely wealthy and well connected, had next to nothing in assets. A few thousand dollars in a bank account. Not a joint account with his wife, as was the custom. He had no investments, which again I felt was odd. His only real asset was the house, which he owned jointly with one Hildegard A. Gold. I hated to admit it, but I couldn't help but wonder what kind of a woman has a name like Hildegard these days. I could only hope that she used a nickname of some kind.

Little money. No investments. I made a mental note to ask his father about his son's occupation. Perhaps that would explain a few things.

The intercom on my desk phone buzzed, and Millie's voice followed.

"Miss Brennan?"

"Yes, Millie." Everyone else in the firm called her Millicent. She had seemed so tickled when I called her Millie that I continued, in spite of the occasional raised brow I received from one of the partners.

"A Miss Barnes on line three for you."

"Thanks, Millie." It took me several moments to remember exactly who Miss Barnes was. I picked up the receiver and pushed the button alongside line three.

"Kate Brennan." I'd been taught long ago to always answer the phone by stating my name, regardless of whether or not I knew who was on the other end of the line.

"I thought you'd given up on family law." Melanie Barnes's voice bristled.

"Excuse me?" I had no idea what Melanie wanted, but I didn't like the tone in her voice.

"I thought you were a corporate attorney now. What are you doing representing someone in a divorce case?"

"Well hello to you too, Mel. Let's not bother with catching up or anything." My tone was sarcastic.

There was a moment's hesitation on her part. "I'm sorry, Kate. How are you?"

I had to laugh. Melanie and I had shared office space and had worked many times together in the past. She was known for being just a bit excitable, and I knew what kind of an effort she was making to calm down.

"I'm well, Melanie. And you?" I was smiling now. I missed Melanie. With all her flaws, Melanie was so much more human than the lawyers that surrounded me now.

"I was just fine until I found out that you're representing a gold-digging bastard in a divorce case. I can't believe you're representing a man, and a son of a bitch to boot."

In spite of the fact that I agreed wholeheartedly with Melanie's assessment of my client's character, I didn't like the tone she was taking with me.

"First of all, Melanie, yes, I am in corporate law now." I spoke each word succinctly. "And second, there's this little thing called attorney-client privilege that doesn't allow me to discuss who I may or may not be representing with anyone outside of a courtroom." I took a deep breath. "You remember attorney-client privilege, don't you?"

"Very funny, Kate." Her voice was tight. "Who you're representing probably wouldn't be any of my business except for the fact that a copy of the divorce petition that you filed on behalf of *your client* was just delivered to my office."

My heart sank. "Don't tell me."

"Mrs. Gold is my client."

Dammit. I was silent as I mulled this over. It was bad enough that I was being forced to represent *anyone* in a divorce case. Worse still that my client was a man. It was against everything I'd ever tried to accomplish in my own practice that I had to represent a man in a divorce case who was using his wife's lesbianism against her. And now, to add insult to injury, I would be going up against an old and dear colleague. A colleague who had fought as hard as I had to preserve the rights of our lesbian clients.

"Are you there?" Melanie's voice was much quieter now.

"I'm here," I sighed.

"Maybe we can try to make the best of a bad situation."

"How's that?" My eyes closed as I pinched the bridge of my nose.

"Maybe we can come up with a settlement that's fair to everyone without shedding any blood."

My laugh was more like a guffaw. "Don't bet on it," I muttered.

"Is he a real prick?"

In spite of myself, I smiled. "You know I can't comment, Mel."

"Off the record." Her voice was almost a whisper.

I looked around my office, as if someone were hiding somewhere and listening. An uneasy feeling came over me. I wouldn't put it past Donald Gold to have my office bugged or my phone tapped.

"My opinion of my client is irrelevant, Melanie." I put on my best business voice. "Why don't we schedule a time to get together and see if we can work out some sort of agreement."

Melanie was quiet. I could imagine her mentally weighing my words. "I'm sorry, Kate. That was very unprofessional of me. When are you free?"

I flipped through my datebook and we compared schedules. Settling on the following Monday, we said a polite good-bye and ended our conversation.

Chapter 8

The ride to Treasured Past was nearly unbearable. Beth and I had debated for nearly an hour about whether or not we should take separate vehicles. As a result we were running late, and once we were on our way I wished that I'd brought my own car.

"Don't worry about it," Beth was saying. "If I have to leave before you're ready to go, then I'm sure you can get a ride home from Annie."

I groaned. "Why are you so intent on pushing us together? She could be married for all I know."

"No ring," she stated happily.

"She might have plans."

"She might." The singsong tone in Beth's voice was driving me crazy. "If she does, then you'll just have to tag along with me. Billy's game won't last more than an hour."

I bit my tongue. Spending an hour watching Beth's son play left field in a Little League game wasn't the worst way I could spend my afternoon. In spite of the efforts of Beth's ex-husband to keep his son away from his mother, it was Billy who had made life almost intolerable for his father by insisting that Beth continue to have a strong role in his young life. Very mature for his nine years, Billy had stood his ground firmly when it came to including his mother in every part of his life. Beth's ex-husband may have won legal custody, but it was Beth who clearly owned Billy's heart.

Even now, the guilt that came over me every time Billy's name was mentioned was palpable. I didn't think I would ever forgive myself for losing Beth's custody battle. My mood sobered.

Beth pretended not to notice. Instead she prattled on about Annie and how good it would be to see her again.

"You know, you keep teasing me about Annie." I turned in my seat to face her squarely. "I think maybe it's *you* who's attracted to her."

Beth's ire wouldn't be raised. "Not my type."

"Oh, why not?" I folded my arms across my chest and pretended not to believe a word.

"You know I like 'em butch." She took her eyes off the road just long enough to slide me a mischievous glance and pat my leg. "Kinda like you."

"I am *not* butch." Beth knew all my buttons, and now she was roaring.

"You are. You may not *look* butch, but everything else about you is."

"I don't believe in that butch-femme thing," I insisted.

"I know. I don't either. But I sure do like to get you going."

I opened my mouth to give her a not-so-subtle piece of my mind, but she cut me off.

"Is this the place?"

I glanced out the window and felt my stomach flutter. "Yep. We're here." I was nervous again.

"Did she tell you where to park?" Every metered parking space was taken.

"She said to pull around back. There's a loading dock or something back there."

Beth navigated her truck down a back alley, and we were surprised to see an oversize doorway at the back of the building. A rough wooden sign hanging above the door proclaimed TREASURED PAST.

"Easy enough," Beth declared. Then she reversed the truck and backed it up until we were just a few feet from the door.

The number of shoppers that were milling about the store amazed me. Annie greeted us warmly.

"You made it," she smiled.

"Sorry we're late," Beth told her. We were supposed to be there before the store opened at noon.

"No problem. I can't really break away right now, but if you two want to unload the furniture in the back, we can move it inside as soon as there's a break." She was brushing a stray strand of hair from her brow.

"Sounds fair to me." Beth was all smiles as we left the store together and unloaded the truck.

It took no time at all, and my dilemma began. It was unthinkable to just leave the furniture outside and make Annie bring everything in herself. But the number of people in the store made it clear to me that it would be a long wait before Annie could take a break.

Beth wasted no time in solving the problem. She waited until Annie had wrapped up a customer's purchase and thanked them before approaching the counter.

"Annie, I hate to do this. But I really need to get to my son's baseball game."

"I didn't know you have a son. What's his name?" Annie's smile was broad.

"Billy," Beth smiled. "Unfortunately, I don't get to spend a lot of time with him, so it's important that I be there."

Annie glanced my way. "Don't worry about it. You two go ahead and take off."

"Oh no," Beth waved her off. "We wouldn't dream of asking you to drag all that stuff in by yourself. Kate can hang around until the end of the day if you wouldn't mind giving her a ride home."

I could feel my face reddening, and I bit my lip. I was sure that Annie would feel like she had been saddled with me. But I was wrong.

"What a wonderful idea." Now she turned her attention to me. "Can I put you to work while you're here?" She was grinning.

"You can certainly try," I told her. "But I'm not promising that I'll be much help."

She let her eyes wander boldly up and then down

my body before nodding firmly. "You look trainable enough."

I pretended that I wasn't embarrassed, but I didn't miss Beth's smirk. Shrugging my shoulders, I refused to meet Beth's eyes. "Then I'm all yours," I told her, knowing that Beth's smirk was turning into a huge grin.

Once Beth had left, I asked Annie whether or not she had anyone to help her in the store. "It seems awfully busy in here for just one person."

"I've had help on and off in the past. But I can't afford to pay much, and it's hard to find someone that you can trust." Her tone was matter-of-fact. She paused to answer a question from a young woman interested in Fiesta ware.

"I'm afraid I'm not going to be much use to you," I told her. "I don't know anything about this stuff."

"That's okay," she said easily. "It would be a big help if you just stay back here behind the counter and greet people for me."

"I think I can manage that. But can't you give me something else just a little more challenging to do?" I couldn't stand feeling useless.

"Sure. Can you work a cash register?"

I didn't want to admit that I never had, so I nodded. It looked simple enough to me.

"Good. Let me show you how we write things up." Annie was all business now, and I focused hard while she showed me how she wrote sales receipts. Every item in the store had a white tag that included an item number, a description of the item, and a price. All the information was written on a two-copy sales receipt. The white copy went to the customer, and the yellow copy was placed in what amounted to a little shoebox under the counter. Each price was entered into the cash register, which calculated the sales tax and the total sale.

The procedure was simple enough, even for a gal like me who had never lived through the rite of passage that most kids do at one time or another. I'd never worn a McDonald's uniform for a single day of my life. Although I did remember a time when, as a preteen, I'd envied the lime-green polyester uniform worn by the girls behind the counter. I remembered the wide round ring that was the zipper pull, and the matching lime-green hat. I'd thought that the outfit was absolutely stunning. It wasn't until years later, when my mother reminded me of how desperately I wanted to wear that uniform, that I laughed until I nearly cried. The thought of hamburger and French-fry grease permeating the polyester outfit made me cringe when I remembered the uniform that I'd wanted so badly.

I was smiling at the memory and only nodded when Annie made some kind of statement before she turned and left me alone behind the counter. I was on my own.

The first two hours were rather uneventful. I managed to muster up a smile whenever a new customer opened the door. I had the checkout procedure mastered after only a couple of people brought their purchases to the counter. After a while, I found myself eagerly fielding questions, which of course I had no idea how to answer. But it gave me legitimate reasons to approach Annie to relay the question of the moment. After several hours, I found that I'd actually been enjoying myself, and was surprised and just a bit disappointed when it was almost time to close the shop.

At about a quarter of five, a gentleman came through the door carrying a large paper sack and approached the counter. He looked to be just a bit older than myself, with premature gray streaks beginning to emerge at his temples. His smile was friendly but hesitant.

"Hi. I don't think I've seen you here before. Did Annie break down and hire someone to help her out?" He placed the paper bag on the counter.

I smiled a bit warily. "I'm actually just helping her out today."

"Is she here?" he asked brightly.

"She's back there somewhere." I pointed to the opposite end of the store. "Would you like me to find her for you?"

He considered the question momentarily. "I think that would be best." He patted the bag that he'd placed on the counter. "I made a purchase awhile back that I need to talk to her about."

I glanced at the paper bag curiously and nodded my head. "Okay. I'll go track her down."

I glanced back at the man only once to make sure he was behaving himself before I found Annie in the farthest aisle, rearranging a display of crockery. She smiled as I approached.

"There's a guy up front that wants to talk to you. He says he bought something awhile back that he needs to discuss with you."

She frowned. "I hope he doesn't want a refund." She sighed and wasted no time in walking to the front of the store. I was close behind.

"Jim. How are you?" She recognized him from behind, and he turned and smiled. I thought he looked nervous.

"I'm fine, Annie. And you?"

"Fine. Just fine." She stepped behind the counter and faced him, the smile warming her face. "What can I do for you?"

"Well, I'm a bit embarrassed about this." He dropped his eyes and began to fidget with the paper bag. "I bought this Eoff and Shepard set a couple of months ago." He opened the bag and pulled out what looked like a tea and coffee set. He placed all four pieces on the counter. "At least I *thought* it was an Eoff and Shepard."

Annie's brow wrinkled as she shook her head. "Jim, I don't think I've ever seen this before. I don't remember ever having it in the shop."

"I know." He almost interrupted her. "I didn't actually see it here in the store," he stammered. He began to fidget, and my curiosity was piqued.

"Your husband sold it to me."

"My —"

"It's a long story."

For a moment I couldn't hear anything above the rushing sound in my ears. Annie was married. I thought my heart would fall right into my stomach.

"So when I saw him I mentioned that I was interesting in finding a particular tea and coffee set by Eoff and Shepard," he was saying. "About two weeks later he called and said he'd managed to run across a set. He even delivered it to my office." He paused long enough to see the frown on Annie's face. "But the problem is, it's not an original. It's a replica. I went to have it appraised for my insurance policy, and I was told that I'd been conned."

Annie looked dumbfounded. I could almost see the wheels turning as she considered his words.

"But, Jim, that transaction has nothing to do with this store. That's between you and —"

"No, unfortunately that's not true." He fumbled as he reached into his back pocket and pulled out a brown leather wallet. "I have the receipt." He unfolded a piece of paper and placed it on the counter in front of Annie. It was undoubtedly one of her receipts, the white copy to be exact.

"You paid six thousand dollars for *this*?" Her voice was incredulous.

"Yes," he nodded. "And it appraised at fifty dollars. I think you can appreciate my concern."

She raised tired eyes to his before dropping them back down to the sales receipt, studying it intently. As if suddenly remembering my presence, her gaze lifted to meet my intense stare, catching me off guard. I couldn't read the thoughts or emotions that rifled her features. She was clearly disturbed, and for a moment I forgot about the fact that I was crestfallen. I excused myself, removing myself from their presence as gracefully as possible.

So much for Beth's matchmaking, my mind was speaking overtime to me. Even my own instincts had been incorrect. I had thought that Annie might actually be interested in me. So much for intuition.

I pretended to be engrossed in a display of butter dishes while my ears strained to hear the conversation between Annie and Jim. It would probably have been classified as eavesdropping if I could have deciphered a word of what they were saying. But I could only hear mumbling.

I picked up a dish and turned it over in my hand, pretending that I wasn't watching as Annie pulled a large, oversize checkbook from underneath the counter and began scribbling a check. Then she was ripping it from the book, her face and voice full of apology as she handed it over to Jim. Her face was the highest shade of red that I had ever seen, and I wasn't sure if it was out of embarrassment or anger.

I didn't approach her immediately. Instead, I busied myself until the last customer had left the store and Annie locked the door behind him. She looked weary as she flipped the sign in the window so that CLOSED appeared to anyone peeking in.

I knew that she wished I wasn't there, and I felt like an intruder invading her personal business. I decided that the best thing to do was pretend that I hadn't witnessed what was probably a very embarrassing moment for her.

"Should we go ahead and move the furniture in?" I asked breezily. "I'm sure you have plenty to do and are probably ready to get me out of your hair."

She was looking in my direction, but she seemed vacant, as though she were really seeing past me. She nodded, and without another word she motioned for me to follow her. I trailed several steps behind, noting the dejected way that her shoulders seemed to sag further with every step.

We moved the furniture from the dock to inside the back corridor of the store in virtual silence. The only time she spoke was to give me direction. "Watch your step on the floorboard here" and "This is a tight corner, you'll have to stay as far right as possible."

"Ready to go?" I could tell that she was forcing a smile as she locked up the store and we headed to her car.

"Nice night," I said lamely.

"Kind of warm," she replied, and I almost laughed. It was mid May. There was no such thing as too warm this early in the year.

Her silence was stony as she drove out of Cambridge and through Watertown on her way to my home in Newton. She pulled into my driveway and finally spoke as she put the transmission into park.

"I'm sorry about what happened back at the store. It was quite embarrassing, and I got flustered." She wasn't looking at me. Instead she stared directly ahead, focused on the garage door.

"Don't apologize. I didn't even understand what was going on," I lied. "And you know that I don't have a clue about who Eoff and Shepard are." I was trying to inject a little humor, and I was rewarded when I caught the slight lifting at the corner of her lips. But she said nothing.

"Do you want to come in?" I finally asked. "You've already eaten the one dish I can prepare, but I can try to throw something together for us."

Her voice was tired. "I would like nothing more than to relax with you this evening." She took a deep breath. "But no, unfortunately. I'm afraid I wouldn't be very good company, and I have quite a bit of work to do." Her voice seemed strained.

"Okay." I wasn't going to push. I reached for the door handle and was about to open it when she interrupted.

"I didn't realize Beth had a little boy." Her voice was quiet and even. "She's not married?"

Annie had no idea that she was opening up one of my wounds. "No, not anymore. She's been divorced for a couple of years now. The whole case was a nightmare, actually. Maybe I'll tell you about it sometime." Why was I telling her this?

Annie was nodding slowly, digesting this.

"Are you and Beth partners?"

"Excuse me?" I couldn't be certain that I'd heard her correctly.

She seemed to falter and appeared to be shocked by her own words. Her eyes met mine, and her smile was uncomfortable.

"I'm sorry, it's none of my business." Her eyes dropped, and she waved the topic aside.

"No. It's okay. I just wasn't sure if I heard you correctly." It crossed my mind again that Annie might be interested in Beth. Then I remembered that she was married.

She looked at me squarely. "I asked if you and Beth are partners."

"I thought that's what you said." My laugh sounded strangled, and I caught my breath as I stared back at her. "No, we're not. But not for a lack of effort on my mother's part." My laugh was hearty.

"Your mother?" For the first time in hours, Annie's smile was genuine.

"Yeah, she adores Beth. My dad too."

"But there's nothing between you?"

Now that was a tough question to answer. "Well, we've known each other most of our lives, so there's plenty between us. But nothing romantic. Not since about the seventh grade, anyway."

"Seventh grade?" Another leading question.

"Yes. We were crazy about each other back then.

62

We experimented a little . . ." I purposely let the sentence trail off.

Annie's smile was lopsided as she nodded. "Experimented, eh? I suppose that's another story that you'll have to tell me about sometime."

I shrugged, enjoying her banter. "Maybe," I said. "I did invite you in."

"I know. I appreciate it. But I really should get some work done tonight. Can I have a rain check?"

"Of course," I nodded, reaching for the door handle once again. Then it struck me. She probably had to get home to her husband. My heart fell again, and then I thought about the confrontation that would probably occur when she walked in the door.

"I didn't know you were married." The words were out before I could stop them.

Her face held no expression. "I'm not. Anymore."

Her words were simple and direct, but said far less than the hard eyes that bore into mine. I felt a tingle somewhere between my heart and my belly and almost shivered. She wasn't married. And the look she was throwing my way told me clearly that it wasn't Beth that she was interested in.

Chapter 9

Melanie Barnes looked better than I'd ever remembered seeing her. She wore a fine summer dress that fit snugly, quite a difference from the tan suit that I was wearing. She was a natural redhead, with the whitest skin and more freckles than I'd ever seen on another human being.

She wrapped thin arms around my neck and gave me a big squeeze when she greeted me.

"Kate, you look so good."

"You mean I look better than I did the last time you saw me," I laughed.

"You were beginning to look like you never went to bed," she admitted. "I'm just glad to see that the change has been good for you."

"It has," I admitted.

The restaurant where we'd arranged to meet was near Copley Plaza in downtown Boston. The café had several tables outside, shaded from the strong sun. We decided to enjoy the fine weather and settled into a corner table, out of the way from most of the other clientele.

We began catching up, Melanie filling me in on how everyone was and how they were doing. We ordered iced tea and waited for our salads to appear.

"How's Beth doing? Do you ever see her?"

"She's doing well. I see her all of the time." It took me a second to realize that the last contact Melanie had with Beth was during Billy's custody battle. She was studying my face carefully, and I knew where her thoughts were going.

"She actually sees quite a bit of Billy, too. Her ex-husband came around after a while. Billy was having a lot of trouble adjusting, and so her ex finally gave in. She doesn't have custody, but they get to spend a lot of time together."

Melanie remained silent, still studying me.

"I'm okay, Melanie," I told her.

"It wasn't your fault, Kate. Judge Leahy is a redneck son of a bitch."

I could see her beginning to get excited, and I did my best to intervene. "I know, Mel. Really. I've forgiven myself for losing the case." I knew as I said the words that I was lying. I could have done more to win custody for Beth. "Beth and I have moved on, and life is good now. Stress free."

She narrowed her green eyes. "You certainly look happier."

"I am. I promise." The waitress rescued us by placing two large salad plates on the table. I waited for her to leave the table before turning back to Melanie.

"So why don't we get down to business?" I watched her closely while I lifted a tomato slice to my lips. "I understand that the only joint property here is a home in Cambridge."

Melanie nodded. "The house originally belonged to my client's parents. She inherited the house when they died about eight years ago."

I completely lost my appetite. "You mean they didn't purchase the home together?"

Melanie shook her head. "She only put his name on the title to keep the peace."

Swallowing hard, I dropped my fork to the table. "That son of a bitch," I muttered.

"Aha." Melanie pointed her fork directly at me. "So you didn't know about the inheritance?"

I shook my head. "I knew that he was an ass. But I actually know very little about him." I was steaming, shaking my head. "I had no idea about the house."

Melanie was carefully quiet, chewing pleasantly on a piece of lettuce. Trying to control my temper was difficult. I was walking a fine line with my old friend. I wanted to rant and rave and scream about the situation I was in, but at the same time I was acutely aware of my professional obligations.

"He wants the house." I was almost growling. "No if's, and's, or but's."

Melanie took another bite of her salad, completely calm. "I'd call that stealing," she said between bites.

"Legal theft, I'm afraid." My stomach was sour. "More like blackmail, actually."

I finally got Melanie's attention. "What do you mean, blackmail?"

"You don't know?"

Melanie shook her head, and I felt a sick kind of thrill at the irony of the situation. "I certainly don't know the details," I began. "But apparently my client witnessed his wife having sex with another woman."

Melanie's grin was sinister. "Good for her, I say."

"Melanie . . ." I was exasperated.

"Sorry." She held up one hand. "I'm aware that my client was caught in a rather compromising position with another woman." Her voice was almost prim.

"In the home that they shared, in *their* bed."

"Which they hadn't shared for *four* years," Melanie interjected.

I studied her closely. "The house or the bed."

"Both." The sound of a carrot crunching between her teeth sounded far too smug. "They were separated."

"For four years?" I was incredulous.

"Yep."

"Legally?"

Melanie paused. "Nope. Got me there." She took her time sipping from her glass of iced tea. "Apparently he couldn't hold a job and kept floating from one thing to another. Finally she'd had enough and threw him out. She wanted a divorce but felt sorry for him." She was chewing happily, watching my reaction. "She should have divorced him back then, and we wouldn't be going through all of this."

Stunned by what I'd learned, I could barely gather

my thoughts enough to figure out where to go from there. I remembered Donald Junior's words to me several weeks before, and repeated them to Melanie.

"He said that he'll ruin her," I said evenly. "He said that if she fights him on the house, he'll make sure that everyone knows that she's a lesbian."

Melanie's thin brows pulled up slowly. "Interesting tactic," she mumbled. "But not totally unexpected." She placed her fork on the table beside her salad plate. "So basically there's no compromise as far as he's concerned."

"No." I shook my head, my lips a careful line.

Melanie studied my face for several moments. "And I'm supposed to take this *compromise* back to my client? If she fights him on the house then he'll out her?"

I nodded, sighing. "That's pretty much the deal," I cringed.

I watched her face register fury before she calmed herself down and shrugged. "I'm not exactly surprised. He sounds like a real loser." She picked up her fork once again. "So how did you get involved with this guy, anyway?"

I closed my eyes and pinched the bridge of my nose. "You know I can't go into that."

"Confidentially, I promise. Just between you and me." She was leaning forward, elbows on the table.

I was embarrassed to admit that I was basically having my arm twisted behind me. "I'm surprised that you didn't figure it out." I fiddled with my fork to avoid her eyes. "Donald Gold's father is a senior partner in my firm."

I could see the wheels spinning in Melanie's mind.

"Brown, Benning, and Gold." She slapped her forehead. "Why didn't I figure that out?" Our eyes met and held for several moments. "Let me guess. You're being forced to take this case."

"More or less." My tone held a touch of sarcasm.

Melanie was shaking her head. "You must be furious."

"More or less," I repeated. "It's not that I'm crazy about my job, but I don't know if I'm ready to throw it away yet just because I'm being asked to represent my boss's son."

"Even if he's a jerk?"

I was frowning. "I've had enough change in my life over the last year. My work has been stable and worry-free."

"Until now," Melanie reminded me.

"Until now." I began to speculate in my mind about my situation at my office.

"Why don't you come back to the center? You know we could always use you on our side."

Just the thought made me shiver. "I can't go back right now. Maybe not ever." Anxiety crept along my spine. "I don't really enjoy what I'm doing right now, Melanie. But the money is unbelievable and I don't get emotionally involved with my clients." My voice was firm. "It's been good for me."

Melanie's chin tilted up as she assessed me once again. "You look like a completely different person from a year ago. It's obviously been a good move for you, Kate. But you should know that we all miss you, and we'd welcome you back with open arms."

My throat hurt as I thought of the women that I'd worked with, the ones I'd represented. I had never felt so many highs — or lows. And now I didn't think that I could ever go back.

Chapter 10

I sat in the car outside my office and counted to
ten. At least twenty times. It wasn't working. I knew
if I walked into the building that I would go directly
to Donald Gold's office. I knew that I would interrupt
whatever he was doing and demand some answers. I
knew I would break every unspoken rule about how a
junior member in a law firm should treat one of the
senior partners.

"Dammit!" My fist struck the steering wheel, and I
instantly regretted the move. "Ouch." I rubbed my
hand, feeling sorry for myself. Why did things

suddenly have to get so difficult? Everything had been going so well. My world had begun to center on my home and personal life. I'd been able to leave my work behind me at the office each day. Now I was in a quandary. Everything about this case seemed so unethical. I was involved for all the wrong reasons, and my stomach was queasy.

I put the key back in the ignition and started the engine. I wasn't about to go upstairs and make a fool of myself by blowing up in front of everyone. I wouldn't give Donald Gold the satisfaction. I'd figure out a solution to my dilemma. Somehow I had to believe that I would be able to make things right.

I drove to Cambridge. I didn't think about the how's or why's. I just drove.

The neighborhood around Treasured Past seemed quiet, and I had no trouble finding a parking space right outside the store.

Without thinking, I opened the car door and swung my feet to the pavement, walking briskly to the front door. I grabbed the doorknob and pulled, surprising myself when the door didn't budge.

Taking a step backward, my eyes moved to the CLOSED sign displayed in the window. Frowning, I read the posted store hours and swore under my breath. CLOSED SUNDAYS AND MONDAYS.

Now what would I do? Not that I had a plan before. But I'd wanted to see Annie. Pouting, I didn't hear the locks snapping open as Annie threw open the door. Then she was standing in the doorway, waving me inside. Her hair was down, a wavy auburn mass just past her shoulders. She turned on one heel, beckoning me to follow.

I stepped inside, and she was already behind the counter, flipping through a brochure and looking distracted. Neither of us had even said hello, and I held back, waiting for her to break the silence. I didn't have to wait long.

"Here." She was folding back a page and holding it up for me to look at. I couldn't help thinking that she didn't seem at all surprised to see me, as if she had expected me to walk through that door when I did. She was pointing to a black-and-white photograph that I couldn't decipher from this distance. "These might be perfect."

I stepped closer, squinting at the poor image of what appeared to be an old sectional bookcase. It was impossible to tell what it was made of or how large it was from the picture, but it appeared to be extremely tall, with multiple sections that must have covered many yards.

I narrowed my eyes, completely lost. I had no idea what she was talking about.

"Perfect for what?" I dared to inquire.

She stared at me for a moment, then blinked hard. "For your great room." Her tone was matter-of-fact as her eyes dropped back to the photograph. "I can't be certain of the dimensions, but I think it would be worth taking a look at."

Her eyes met mine again, and this time I recognized the look that I'd seen on her face so often before. The same look that I knew showed on my own face whenever I discovered a piece of antique furniture that I had to have.

"What's your budget?"

I was holding back my smile. "I didn't know I had one," I told her, trying to keep from laughing.

Apparently I wasn't doing a very good job of hiding my reaction, because her eyes floated over my face and then seemed to come into focus. Her smile was slow.

"Hi." She drew the single syllable out slowly, her voice low. "I'm glad to see you." The way her eyes were sparkling made my stomach flutter.

"Hi." I returned her grin. "You don't seem surprised to see me."

"You're right." Her eyes stayed on mine as she contemplated her reply. "I know this probably sounds silly, but somehow I just expected you to be here." Her lashes fluttered as she glanced at the brochure she held in one hand. "I was sitting here thinking about you and thinking what a good fit these shelves might be in your house. I glanced up and there you were, almost as though I conjured you up."

I didn't know how to respond. She seemed almost magical as she stood there, full of enchantment and casting a spell over me.

"So forgive me," she continued when I didn't speak. "What brings you here?" The change in her voice was subtle, as though she regretted what she had just said.

I could only shrug. "I'm not sure exactly," I admitted. "I had a lousy day at work, and I had to get away. The next thing I knew I was parked outside your store."

Annie studied me carefully, eyes narrowing for an instant. I thought about what I was saying, about what it might mean that it was Annie that I had wanted to see.

I spoke my thoughts aloud. "I guess I just wanted to see you." My face grew hot as I risked the words.

She didn't respond right away, but rather took a moment, as if to digest my words and decide whether they had any meaning. "I'm glad," she said simply.

We watched each other awkwardly until she glanced at her watch and then broke the silence. "So you're playing hooky. We should be having fun then, I suppose." Her smile warmed me.

"Sounds perfect to me." I could almost guess where the conversation was leading. I nodded toward the brochure in her hand. "Do you have something in mind?"

"Are you up for an auction? There's one over at the Legion Hall that starts at seven." She glanced quickly at her watch again. "We could wander over there and take a look to see if there's anything interesting. These shelves might be perfect in your house, but we should probably get some measurements first."

I laughed. "You just want me to spend more money."

Her eyes grew larger. "No, that's not it. I'm sorry. I shouldn't assume —"

"I'm kidding," I interrupted her. "I just can't believe you've given that room a second thought. No one else has shown any interest."

"Are you kidding? Nothing would make me happier than to help you redesign and decorate that room." Her eyes were lit with enthusiasm. "I have this visual image of what I'd do with it." She stared off in the distance, and I found myself unable to control my smile.

"Would you really want to help me with it?" I

asked. "I just wouldn't think of asking anyone to do it. Every time I stare into that room I just feel so overwhelmed."

"Oh, Kate. There's so much you could do in there. I have so many ideas. I know I should probably stay out of your business, but I just can't help it."

The thought of having Annie in my home, helping me decorate, made my heart sing. "I would love to have your help. I don't even know where to start."

"Really?"

"But we'd have to agree on payment."

"Absolutely not."

"But it will take so much time. You've surely got better things to do."

"I can't take any money, Kate." She placed both hands on her hips. "It would be pure enjoyment for me. I would have so much fun. And it would be a good distraction for me."

I raised an eyebrow. "A distraction from what?"

She seemed to stammer. "Oh, from the store. From antiquing. Summer is almost here, and that's our slow season."

I don't think I quite believed her, but decided to let it pass. "We would still have to come up with some kind of payment, Annie. I just wouldn't feel good about you doing so much work for nothing."

Annie brushed me aside again. "It's not necessary, Kate. Besides, if you pay me then I'll think of it as a job instead of a fun project." She pulled her lips together adamantly. "Besides, you'll already be spending a ton of money on the design and improvements." Her smile was wicked. "I've been known to have expensive tastes when I'm spending someone else's money."

I laughed and regarded her for a few moments, thinking again about what it would be like to have her spending so much time in my home. "I guess I'll just have to buy you a present, then. To thank you for your work."

I thought I detected a slight blush on her cheeks. "Don't thank me yet. You may not like what I do."

I sighed, completely charmed. "I can't imagine that, Annie," I gushed, then blanched as I realized what I was thinking about. No use fighting it or denying it any longer. All I wanted at that moment was to worm my way into Annie Walsh's heart.

"We'll see." She interrupted my thoughts. "Does that mean we have a deal?"

I nodded, tongue-tied again.

"Good." She reached under the counter and pulled out a tape measure. "Let's go take some measurements. Then we can check out the auction and see what they have."

Chapter 11

The bookcases were enormous but would have fit perfectly except for the fact that they were in terrible shape. Annie wrinkled her nose when she inspected them, obviously disappointed.

"We would have to restore them. There're so many pieces missing, and someone obviously tried to strip this section and never bothered to finish it. We would have to strip the entire thing down." She was trying to maintain her enthusiasm, but it was clear that her heart wasn't in it. "It's your choice. But I think they would be a lot of work."

It was an easy decision for me. "I think I'll have to pass on this one. This thing has *regret* written all over it."

"You mean you'd regret it if you brought it home."

"Exactly. It would be a lot of trouble just getting it to the house. Not to mention all the work it needs." I shook my head. "I think we'll have to keep looking."

Annie nodded, already taking another glance around the crowded room. "I don't see anything in here that trips my trigger. How about you?"

I shook my head. Everything felt dirty. No one had taken the time and energy to clean the items before the auction. I glanced around one last time to be sure. "Nothing," I told her.

She nodded and began strolling toward the exit. It was early yet, barely five o'clock. We had left my car back at my house, and my mind began to race frantically. I didn't want my time with Annie to end.

"Would you like to go to dinner?" I asked her as we stepped outside.

I expected her to hesitate, but she didn't. "Sounds good. I'm quite hungry, actually. Where shall we go?"

"Do you like pizza?"

"Please." She rolled her eyes dramatically. "I can't get enough of it. Can we?"

"Of course. There's a great little place around the corner from my house." I slid her a sheepish look. "I actually get takeout from there at least twice a week."

Annie laughed. "A woman after my own heart."

Exactly. I muttered the word under my breath.

We ate in my living room, curled up on the single forest-green couch while Annie stared longingly into the great room.

"I have so many ideas that I don't know where to start," she sighed, wiping a napkin across her lips.

"Actually, I'd always thought that I should hire a contractor to build shelving into the wall." I finished the last slice of pizza and felt completely satisfied. "There's so much floor space that you could lose a foot or two all the way around the perimeter and you wouldn't even notice."

Annie threw me an indescribable look. I could see her mind was racing as she jumped to her feet. "That's it." She covered the few steps to the glass doorway and stepped inside the other room. Walking to the center, she raised her eyes to each corner of the ceiling.

"You have enough room for an entire library in here." She turned as I came up from behind to join her. "You could line that entire interior wall with built-in shelving. The molding would have to be duplicated to match the rest of the house, but it could be done." She wrinkled her nose. "Do you like the white paint?"

I shook my head. "I'd prefer natural wood. The walls I'm not certain about."

Satisfied, she nodded and turned to the outside wall, arms folded across her chest.

"These windows are wonderful. You could take advantage of the light coming in by putting in a window seat. Nothing too extravagant. Simple but in keeping with the woodwork in the rest of the room."

She continued to describe her vision until I could almost see the room transform before me. I was nodding, agreeing with her, watching the enthusiasm grow on her face.

"It's a great idea," I told her. "What else?"

She turned immediately to the far end of the room where an old stone fireplace was centered in the wall. At some point someone had painted it the same white color as the walls.

"The fireplace is beautiful. I bet that the stones underneath the paint would be perfect if we could strip it off. Does the fireplace work?"

I shrugged. "I've never tried it."

"You should probably get it checked out. I imagine it would make a big difference in what you decide to do with it if you couldn't actually use it."

"That makes sense." I studied the imposing stone mantel, trying to imagine what it might look like if the cold dark center below it was bright with flame.

"Wouldn't it be nice to have a cozy rug near the fireplace, with a soft, comfy couch?"

I nodded. "I love it. You have a wonderful eye."

Annie focused on me once again. "Do you think so?"

"Yes. Everything sounds beautiful. But I don't have a clue about where to start."

Annie's eyebrows pulled together as she thought. "Let me make a couple of phone calls. You need to get some estimates from people who are familiar with doing renovations. You don't want some hack to come in here and put up traditional woodwork. Whoever does it will have to be able to replicate what's currently here." She walked toward me and frowned. "This is going to be expensive."

"It sounds like it," I told her.

She screwed up her face in an apologetic cringe. "Do you have a budget in mind?"

"I do have a limited bank account." I laughed.

"But let's start putting some numbers together and see what we come up with."

"Really?" She seemed barely able to contain herself.

"If you're sure you really want to do this."

"Kate, this is wonderful." She stepped forward, wrapping her arms around my neck and squeezing me tightly. I know the hug only lasted a few seonds, but it felt as though time was suspended. The clean, fresh scent of her hair filled my nose as I took one deep breath. The unexpected feel of her arms around me and the closeness of her body against mine left me unable to breathe.

When she finally released me, it wasn't until I saw the smile on her face that I could finally exhale. The sound of the air leaving my lungs was like a heavy, yearning sigh.

Chapter 12

My strategy was simple. Say nothing to Donald about my meeting with Melanie. Give no indication of what I'd learned at all. Nearly weeks had passed since our meeting, and I knew that Donald was beginning to stew. It wasn't like him not to stop in and ask for a status report on where his son's case was headed. But I knew that he was waiting for me to come to him, and I refused.

I had spoken with Donald Junior only once since our initial meeting, to let him know that a court date had been set for mid August, a full ten weeks away. I mentioned that I had met with his wife's lawyer and that we had discussed terms of the settlement but had reached no conclusions.

He reminded me again that he wouldn't settle for anything less than the value of the house. Funny. The way he'd phrased it, it sounded as though he wasn't really interested in the house itself. Just the price that it would fetch and the money it would put in his pocket.

I had wondered how long it would take Donald to find his way into my office. But after three weeks, I didn't have to wait any longer.

"Am I interrupting?" Donald's white hair was in stark contrast with his tanned skin. I knew that his question was a mere formality, and that he didn't give a damn whether he was interrupting me or not.

"Come in," I told him, my smile tight and fixed. *Here we go.*

He didn't shut the door behind him, and I was secretly encouraged. At least he would think twice before raising his voice.

"How are we doing?" Another attempt to be courteous. But I wasn't going to be lulled.

"Just fine," I told him, careful to keep my voice light.

He smiled and nodded before folding himself into one of the two overstuffed armchairs that faced my desk.

"Thought I'd stop in and see how Donald's case is coming along." He paused briefly. "Should I be worried about the fact that you haven't given me an update in several weeks?"

"Not at all." I put on my best professional demeanor. "There just isn't much of an update to give you. The court date has been set for August thirteenth." I paused. More just to make him wait than for any other reason. "I met with the other attorney and presented your son's wishes about the house." I purposely stopped at that point to make him ask for more information.

"And?" I could see his impatience, even though he was struggling to hide it. "Did they agree to our terms?"

You mean, did they agree to be blackmailed? I wanted to say the words aloud but held back. I still had several more cards to play.

"The attorney said that she would discuss it with her client. We're scheduled to meet again a week from Thursday."

Donald nodded, and I took the opportunity to soften my voice and play the role of the helpless, ignorant female.

"Donald. I don't think I ever asked you. What does your son do for a living?"

The crease between his brows deepened. "He's in real estate."

Real estate. How appropriate. "Is he quite successful, then?" I knew I was walking a fine line by starting this line of questioning.

"I don't really see where that's any of your business," he snapped, the ferocity of his tone surprising me.

Bingo. I'd hit a sore spot. *This could get interesting.*

I forced my voice to remain calm, even casual. "Well, Donald, I agree that on a personal level, your son's financial affairs are none of my business. But as his attorney, I must admit that I'm feeling a bit at a loss. It's as though there are some important pieces of information that are missing for me." I dropped my voice to a hushed tone. "My concern is that some of this information might surface when we get inside that courtroom."

"And I'm assuming that you'll never let this case get that far. I'm paying you to make sure that this is settled before it gets to a judge." His voice was firm and brittle.

I remained calm, spreading my palms on the desktop. "I understand your wishes, sir. But my concern is that your son's wife seems to be reluctant to settle under his terms. If she refuses to settle, then I'm going to be ill prepared to explain to a judge why your son is so deserving of their home."

Donald was steaming, and I wasn't sure if I should be pleased with myself, or if I should fear for my life. Nostrils flaring, he was clenching his jaw.

"Your job is to make sure it never gets that far." He was repeating himself. Could it be that he'd never considered that he would have to explain what a failure his son was to me, and for the public record?

"I understand that, sir." My voice was respectful but firm. "But let's assume for a moment that this gets before a judge. How am I supposed to explain to him or her that your son deserves to own a house that he hasn't lived in for four years?"

I fully expected to see steam coming from his ears.

"How did you find out about that?" he snarled.

He'd finally managed to insult me. The sweetness left my voice.

"Did you really expect that I wouldn't do my homework?" I was incredulous. "Is that why you gave me this case? Because you have such a low opinion of my work and abilities that you thought I'd walk through this blindly without asking questions?"

"Of course not." Donald began to back-pedal. "Your work is nothing short of extraordinary. I wanted the best possible attorney to represent my son. That's why I came to you."

Bullshit. I struggled to hold my tongue, and he seemed to interpret my hesitance as acquiescence. *As if I would believe one word of your flattery.*

"There's a significant bonus waiting for you if you're successful with this." His voice had grown quiet, and I could see that he believed he had gained the upper hand so easily.

"And I appreciate that, sir." I'd managed to regain control. "But I think that you should be prepared to hear some pretty ugly words if this goes to court."

He was staring at me, jaw working again, but saying nothing. I took his silence as encouragement to continue.

"I understand that you and your son believe that you have a firm ground to stand on. But surely you know that others might be inclined to label your terms as blackmail." It felt so good to say these words. "Particularly in light of the fact that your son hasn't even been living in the house."

Donald's face was a twisted frown. I couldn't tell if he was furious with me or perhaps his son.

"If this gets in front of a judge, I can guarantee you that this information will come out. I can promise you that the opposition will label it blackmail. And I can also promise you that a judge will take a look at all the *facts*, including the fact that the house was *inherited* by your son's wife from her *parents*." I took a deep breath for emphasis. "And that judge will have a very hard time justifying why your son deserves that house."

Ha. Surely he would see the mistake he was making and change his mind. Surely he would think it better to put his tail between his legs than face the wrath of a judge.

His jaw stopped working as he held my gaze squarely. His smile was slow to unwind on his lips. Green eyes narrowed as he leaned back in his chair, and the smile turned into a self-satisfied sneer.

"And there's where you're wrong, my dear."

I tried to steady myself. This wasn't going as planned.

He leaned forward, as if to share a secret for my ears alone. "I've been in this business a very long time, my dear."

If he called me *my dear* one more time, I might be tempted to slap him.

"I know every judge in this county, and there isn't one who doesn't owe me a favor of some kind." I thought he would burst the button of his overstarched shirt as he puffed himself all up. "So you see, my dear, this case getting in front of a judge is the least of my worries."

He stood up now, dismissing me and getting the final word. "Just do your job, and I'll make it worth your while. Stop asking questions, and do your best to get this thing settled quickly." He paused as his hand reached for the doorknob. "Do we understand each other?"

Deflated, I did my best to hide my disappointment and disbelief, carefully toeing the company line.

"We do, sir," I told him, and was relieved to watch his back retreat from my office.

Shoulders sagging, I let myself fall against the back of my chair. Closing my eyes, I wondered how I ever thought I could win this battle.

Chapter 13

Mondays had become my favorite weekday. For the past few weeks, I'd come home on Mondays to find Annie in my home. At first there had been meetings with contractors. She had wasted no time in gathering bids and speaking with a number of professionals until she had settled on the best company for the job.

We had gone over budgets, specifications, schedules, and blueprints until we'd come up with a plan we both loved and a price that I could swallow.

Annie apparently had friends in all the right places, because the construction company wasted no time in delivering lumber and setting up shop in my soon-to-be library. On Mondays, she was there to supervise and provide direction when I was at work. And nearly every weeknight she showed up on my doorstep, a smile on her face and an eagerness to see what had been accomplished during the day.

Today when I arrived, she was sitting cross-legged on the floor in front of the window, carefully stripping away the layers of paint that previous owners had applied to the woodwork.

She wore overalls and a painter's cap turned sideways so that it was neither forward or backward. She must not have heard me come in the door, and I slipped off my shoes before padding quietly into the room behind her.

I waited until I was about three steps behind her before I spoke.

"Aren't we paying someone else an awful lot of money to do that?" The work was tedious. She was gently sweeping away some of the dirt and grit from within the groove of the woodwork.

The face that she turned to me was warm and smiling. "You're right. You *are* paying someone too much to do this for you." She shrugged, her head tilting until one shoulder touched the bill of her cap. "But I can't resist. I can't tell you how much I love working like this." She turned back to her work and brushed it lightly with a stiff brush.

"They got a lot done today. Did you see that the structure is in place for the bookshelves?"

I took a moment to turn and survey the far wall. Sure enough, the shelves had been framed. All traces of the white wall had been covered with rich cherry wood. None of the shelves or decorative molding was in place, but the structure was there. Annie's vision was coming alive before my eyes.

"Wow. It looks really nice, doesn't it?"

Annie had uncurled herself from the floor and now stood beside me. "It's certainly taking shape."

She was close enough that I could smell the freshness of her hair, something I'd also grown used to and come to cherish and agonize over at the same time. It was all I could do to hold back. I could no longer count the number of times I'd wanted to reach out and take the pins from her hair. I yearned to watch it fall, to see just how long it was, and just how the wild curls would frame her face. But I did nothing. I just watched her from a distance, cherishing the moments when she was as close as she was now, and fantasizing about what it might be like to hold her close.

I realized with a start that Annie was looking at me curiously. I must have been staring again.

"Are you okay?" she asked.

"Of course," I recovered.

"You look distracted," she persisted.

"Maybe a little," I admitted.

"Work?" she asked.

I groaned. "Maybe. A case I'm working on is frustrating the hell out of me."

"I'm sorry." Her brows drew together in a look of concern. We rarely talked about my work. Partly because I wanted to leave everything behind at the office. But partly too, I suspected, because Annie seemed to hold a certain distaste for my profession.

I waved away her concern. "I don't even want to

think about it," I told her. "Can you stay for dinner? I thought I'd go change and we could order out. Maybe Chinese?"

"Sounds lovely," she smiled.

I studied her face, noting the tiny crinkles at the corners of her eyes before shaking myself and heading to my bedroom.

I changed into shorts and a T-shirt, returning to find Annie standing before the window that she had been working on before. Her arms were folded loosely against her chest as she leaned against the window sill, staring out into the fading light. The cap she'd worn earlier was now discarded on the floor at her feet. She looked so thoughtful and distant that I didn't want to disturb her.

I stopped just inside the door to watch her, my heart rising to my throat as I traced the outline of her profile with my eyes.

"I went ahead and ordered dinner. I hope you don't mind." Her voice sounded as distant as her gaze. She kept her eyes focused on some faraway target.

The sound of her voice almost frightened me. I'd never heard her sound so quiet. She sounded depressed. Almost troubled.

"Can I ask you something?" she asked quietly.

For some inexplicable reason, my heart was pounding as I answered. "Of course."

She didn't speak right away, and I reasoned that she needed encouragement. So I walked farther into the room to join her. I settled myself against the window sill on the opposite side of the window. A good three feet separated us.

Now that I was closer, I could see that her cheeks were flushed, as if she were embarrassed.

"Annie?" I inquired gently, watching the eyes that she kept so carefully from mine.

She was smiling, but it was a wry smile. She hesitated, taking a deep breath and sighing loudly before speaking.

"Are you seeing anyone right now?" She continued to stare out the window.

My heart thumped wildly. My laughter was born of nervous tension. "You're here every day. So you tell me. Am I seeing anybody?"

I was willing her to meet my gaze, but her refusal was steady. Tension hung in the air between us, and I hoped wildly that her question meant that she was interested in me.

She was struggling with her response, and I could feel her anguish and hesitation. Again a heavy sigh escaped her before she spoke.

"I guess that means that the only person you're seeing is me." Her eyes darted my way before returning to their faraway stare. I thought my heart would stop beating entirely.

Did she say what I think she said? My mind was racing as wildly as my heart, jumping from one thought to the next. Silence stretched, and I could see Annie's expression falter. She was so nervous.

"Every chance I get." I told her the truth. Heart palpitating, I took a gulp of air. "And if I had it my way, I'd see you even more."

Now it was my turn to be nervous. I watched her closely, praying that I'd said the right thing. That I'd read her correctly and hadn't just made a total ass out of myself.

Her expression cleared, a small smile finding her lips as relief spread over her. Then she was shaking her head slowly, still apparently unable to look me in the eye.

"Annie?" My voice sounded meek.

She continued to stare outside as she finally spoke. "I'm here with you every day, Kate, and it's all I can do to keep my distance." Her lips curled softly. "I keep hoping that maybe you've felt it too. That you feel the same way

"I do." My voice grew steady as my heart soared.

Silence. Then finally she raised her eyes to mine. The width of the window was between us, and all I wanted to do was close the gap.

I could see the nervous energy in her eyes.

"Really?" The word was nearly a whisper.

"Really." I was smiling now, full of confidence.

Her eyes were on my smile, and I watched as her lips finally curled shyly.

"Then why didn't you tell me?" She was growing bold, almost playful.

My face blanched. "Too scared, number one."

She studied me. "And number two?" Her head tilted to one side.

I hesitated. "When I learned that you had been married, I thought maybe that you were straight. Nothing's worse than approaching a straight woman and getting rejected."

She considered my words. "I suppose that's so. But I thought that I was telling you every which way that I was interested in you."

"Except for telling me straight out," I interjected.

"Of course not." She shook her head. "Too scared."

I laughed. We'd both been too scared.

Now we looked at each other, awkwardly dropping our eyes, uncertain what to do next.

I raised a hand as if to reach out to her, and I was surprised to see her almost flinch. She seemed more nervous than ever.

I studied her features, confused and uncertain. Then a thought occurred to me.

"Annie, have you ever been with a woman?"

She blanched again before looking me in the eye. "Yes, I have." She raised her chin defiantly. "Exactly one." She paused before grinning mischievously. "Why? Do I look like a rookie?"

My laughter was full and honest.

"Actually, yeah. I don't know many lesbians who look like you."

She frowned. "That's ridiculous, isn't it?"

"Probably," I admitted.

"Not to mention that you're stereotyping," she reprimanded me, lifting a finger and waving it in my direction.

I just laughed. Then our eyes caught and held, and the laughter was replaced with the thick tension.

"So what are we going to do about this?" she asked.

I contemplated her for several moments, wanting nothing more than to wrap my arms around her and pull her close. But something told me that would be the wrong approach.

"Would you like to go out on a date?" My eyebrows rose hopefully.

"I thought that's what we've *been* doing." The sound of her laughter sent a little shiver down my chest. I could hardly believe that we'd gotten this far.

"It kind of feels that way, doesn't it?"

She wrinkled her nose and agreed with me.

"How about we make a real date? For Friday," I suggested.

She was shaking her head. "No good. I've got to come over here every night to see how the workmen are doing, and the tension would be nearly unbearable." She was clearly joking now, confident.

"Okay," I stammered while my mind searched for a quick and witty solution. But I came up with nothing. Shrugging my shoulders, I lifted both hands in the air, palms upward. "Do you have any suggestions?"

Her brows pulled together and she frowned briefly before lifting her eyes back to mine. They were almost sultry.

"Why don't you just come over here and kiss me?"

I thought a dart had pierced my chest. Stomach fluttering, I tried my best to hide my nervousness.

"Command performance, eh? That's kind of tough."

"I'll bet you do quite well under pressure." Her grin was something close to wicked as she slowly pushed herself away from the window and covered the few steps between us.

I was aware that my smile had faltered as she drew within inches of my face. Her smile too had vanished, and I wasn't sure if the beating heart that I heard was hers or my own.

With careful, purposeful slowness, she raised a hand to the side of my face. With two fingers, she tucked a strand of hair behind my ear before letting the palm of her hand come to rest against my cheek.

Instinctively, my lips turned and found the soft center of her palm. Our eyes locked as I continued to let my lips caress her skin. A moment ago I hadn't thought that I'd be able to kiss her, but now the familiar ache was settling in my belly, and the tension in our locked gaze was mounting.

My left hand covered hers, and I slowly lifted her hand from my mouth as my other hand slipped behind her waist. I didn't have to urge her any closer, because before I knew it she was in my arms, her soft, moist lips seeking mine. Surely I had died and gone to heaven.

Chapter 14

I did something the next morning that I don't think I'd done since college. I called in sick. After waking up to find Annie curled around me, I knew that there was no way that I was going to leave her to go in to the office.

We lounged in bed until midmorning, kissing and touching and exploring each other's body as if neither of us had ever been with another woman. Our kisses were slow. Delicate and delicious.

"If I had known this would be so good, I wouldn't

have waited so long to seduce you." Annie murmured the words against my ear as the softness of her body pressed down into mine.

"*You* seduced *me*?" I placed my hands on her shoulders and pushed her away playfully. I'd taken the pins from her hair early the night before, and now the heavy curls created a sheet of darkness against the bright sunlight that shone in the room.

Now she rolled to her back and I followed, lying beside her and propping my head up in one hand.

"I had to," she shrugged. "You were taking so much sweet time that I figured you'd never get around to doing it." She was grinning. "I had no idea you were so shy."

"I'm not so shy anymore." I grinned.

"No, you're not," she agreed. Her smile grew more serious as she lifted a finger and traced around my mouth. "I can't tell you how badly I wanted this to happen."

"Really? When did you decide all of this?"

She didn't have to think about her reply. "The night at your parents' house, during the auction. I'd always thought you were attractive before that. But you'd been my adversary on so many occasions." She pinched my backside gently for emphasis, making me grin. "But that night I knew that I could really grow to care for you if I had the chance." She was tracing my collarbone with one finger. "What about you?"

I smiled, remembering. "I'm not sure, exactly. But Beth knew I was attracted to you long before I was willing to admit it."

"Beth?" Annie seemed surprised.

I nodded. "She was the one that kept pushing me toward you."

"Really?" Annie was grinning. "Remind me to thank her."

"I will. But I don't know if I can take her saying *I told you so.*"

We both heard rumbling from the floor below, and we picked up our heads. It took me a moment to recognize the sounds. "Oh my god. The construction crew. So much for taking the day off."

Annie just laughed and glanced at the bedside clock. "I should probably get into the shop anyway," she sighed. "Why don't you come with me? I could use your help with a few things. You could help me move a few things around and create some new displays."

The thought actually sounded fun. "You just want me for my brute strength," I teased.

Annie gave me a smoldering look. "If that's all I wanted you for, honey, I'd hire me some big burly men. I have many other plans for you in mind."

Her words sent a chill down my spine. I could hardly wait.

Our lives began to fall into a pattern. Annie continued to show up on my doorstep every evening, where she would inspect the work done during the day before joining me for dinner and long conversations. Occasionally, she would leave at the end of the evening to return to her home. But more often than not, we ended up curled around each other in bed, and she wouldn't leave until after daylight.

On Saturdays, I joined her at the shop where I learned more and more about the business and the world of antiquing. I learned even more on Sundays, when we would often go to the shop and take care of all of the things that couldn't be done during the week — bookkeeping and inventory and rearranging displays. Then we reviewed upcoming auctions and events and went through the local newspapers in search of potential bargains. I'd had no idea that there was so much work involved.

We came close to having our first argument when it was time to reconcile the books for Treasured Past at the end of June. After spending hours trying to understand the scribbles in the inventory and sales ledger that Annie kept, I finally convinced her to let me put it all on a computer.

"I hate computers," she insisted, lifting her chin defiantly.

I stared at her, unflinching. "Do you have a computer?" I asked.

"No." Her tone was firm.

"Have you ever worked on one?" I asked.

"No." Again her tone was adamant.

I wanted to giggle, but held back and tried the logical approach. "What if I could put all this information into a simple database that would let you maintain your inventory all in one place?"

"It's all in one place now." She tapped her finger on the green-lined ledger book that I had been fighting with for many hours.

"Okay," I began slowly. "But what if I could make it easier to manage. What if I could put your entire inventory in a database and put all your accounting into a single system." I tried my best to reason with her. "You wouldn't have to spend so much time at the end of each month trying to reconcile everything."

She seemed to hesitate, so I took the opening and

continued. "You would know every single day exactly where you stand financially, what seems to be selling, what you need to add to your inventory . . ."

"But I don't know anything about computers." Her voice had given way to anxiety and frustration.

"I can teach you, Annie."

She was wrinkling her nose. "My accountant would certainly be happier." She sighed. "She's been after me to automate everything for at least two years now." She dropped her eyes and pouted. "I hate change," she growled quietly. "And what if I'm an idiot and can't learn this computer stuff?"

"I'm very patient, Annie." My smile was slow. "And a good teacher, I promise."

Annie lifted her brow. "I imagine you are," she grinned.

So I set about the task of buying a computer and printer and setting it up in the shop. My mission was first finding the perfect software to handle everything we wanted, and converting all the inventory and bookkeeping to the new system. Our evenings shifted as I came straight to Treasured Past after work each day, picking up where I'd left off the day before.

Annie complained that I'd become no fun, but I kept telling her it was temporary. But from the little ways she would look over my shoulder or answer a question when I couldn't decipher the scribbles in one of her ledgers, I could tell that she was thankful. She was also catching up in other areas, no longer glancing through the auction announcements and dealer inventories, but actually going out and making purchases to bring back to the shop.

Along with the construction of the great room moving full-steam ahead, life had become full. So much so that my work at the office was suffering. I knew that I was only doing enough to get by, and knew I also that I didn't even care.

But Donald Gold cared.

"What are you working on these days?" His voice startled me as his large frame filled the doorway to my office.

I assumed he was really inquiring about his son's case, and responded in kind.

"I'm still working on your son's case. I'm meeting again with his attorney next week to try to reach a settlement one more time."

He seemed to chew on this and frowned.

"Working on my son's case is very important to me, I assure you," he began. "But it's certainly not a full-time job." His voice was flat and sarcastic. "What else are you working on?"

He had succeeded in scattering my nerves. "I'm finishing up the petition for the Pritchard case," I stuttered.

"That should have been done two weeks ago," he snapped. His nostrils were flaring, and I could feel his anger from across the room. "You need to start putting whatever it is that's got you so occupied aside and get your head back in the game."

He just stared at me, and I swallowed hard, unable to find a reply. "Do I make myself clear?"

"Yes sir." I managed to squeak the words out and knew they did nothing on my behalf at all. Donald's frown deepened before he turned and walked away. The silence was deafening.

He had managed to shock me into alertness. He was right, of course. I hadn't accomplished much of anything in weeks. Everything had changed so much, what with the construction, the shop, the book-keeping . . . and Annie. That was the difference. Annie had made a tremendous difference in my life. But it was already a little crazy. Both of us seemed to be running full-speed ahead, immersing ourselves in each other's lives.

I rubbed my eyes. The really crazy thing was that I had no idea where all this was heading. For all the time we spent together, I really had no idea how she felt about me, or about us. Not that I'd volunteered many feelings to her, I reminded myself. But it did feel strange to be rearranging my life so much when I had no idea where it was all heading.

And I still knew so very little about her. She never spoke of the past, and while I was admittedly curious, there never seemed to be the opportunity to ask her about anything specifically. So I decided that there would be plenty of time to get to know her better, to understand how she'd become the woman that she was.

I rubbed my eyes again and let out a long sigh. I had to do something about work, but I didn't even know where to start. I knew that I had to find some balance, that it wasn't healthy to be investing so much of myself into Annie.

Annie. I smiled when I thought of her, and how much she had changed my life in such a short time. To hell with Donald Gold, I decided. He and his law firm had little to do with my future.

Chapter 15

I couldn't make sense of what I was looking at. The description in the ledger next to the February 12 entry said *RC Plat F.D. REPL — $??.* I knew I'd seen the same phrase *RC Plat F.D.* somewhere else, but couldn't remember where. To make matters worse, it didn't even look like Annie's handwriting, which I'd gotten rather good at deciphering.

I had no idea what an *RC Flat F.D.* was, or how much to enter as the sale price for the item, and I was growing frustrated. Normally I would have kept going and moved on to the next item, except that I'd already moved past it twice and was ready to reconcile the month. Annie was out at an auction, and I was irritated that I wouldn't be able to finish. So far I'd completed every other month through June, and February was the only thing that got in the way of completing the project. I wanted so badly to be able to finish up and begin to show Annie how to keep track of things going forward.

"Ah." I actually said the word aloud as I knelt down and searched the shelves below the counter. Annie kept copies of all the receipts in shoeboxes under the counter. All I had to do was find the copy and enter in the amount. Simple enough.

Except that the receipt number wasn't in its proper place. So I had to go through each receipt from the box marked February, until I finally found the copy near the bottom. Thirty-eight dollars. Mission accomplished, I put the box back where I'd found it and turned back to the computer and typed in the amount. A few button pushes and mouse clicks later, I ran some reports and was surprised by the results. I was off by thirty-eight dollars. *Dammit*. The cash-register receipts didn't match up to the entries in the ledger.

"Hi." I heard Annie's voice at the same time that I heard the jingle of the bell above the door.

"Hi." I wasted no time in rounding the corner and pulling her into a big hug. "How did it go?"

She groaned in reply. "A waste of time, really. Everything was in such lousy shape, and I just don't have the time or the energy or the patience to do any major restoration work." She kissed me quickly.

"So you're empty handed?" I asked.

"Afraid so," she sighed. "How's it going with you?

Have you tamed the beast yet?" We had begun to refer to the project that I'd undertaken as simply *the beast.*

"I'm almost done." I had to temper my enthusiasm. "I've got everything balanced except for February. Do you think if I showed you something you might be able to figure it out?"

"Does it have to do with math?" she mocked, and I laughed.

"Only a little bit," I assured her. "There's just this one entry that I'm having trouble with." I walked to the other side of the counter and turned the ledger around so that she could read it. She leaned in for a close inspection as I began to ramble.

"Number twenty-three-fourteen, see?" I pointed to the entry. "There's no price beside it, and so I dug up the pink copy."

She raised her eyes to mine quickly, all traces of the previous smile now gone. "Did you find it?"

"Yeah." I squatted down and lifted the lid from the shoebox, removing the receipt. She took it from my hands and stared at it hard.

"Thirty-eight dollars." Her voice sounded hollow.

"Yeah. So I thought I was all set except that after I entered the amount, I was off for the month by thirty-eight dollars." I watched the steady frown grow on her lips, and I wished I hadn't brought any of this up.

"It's no big deal, really. Your cash deposits are just off by thirty-eight dollars for the month. That's all." I tried to sound lighthearted, but knew that my attempts were failing. Annie was upset. Her facial expression and body language were screaming volumes.

"Annie. It's only thirty-eight dollars. No big deal."

She was ignoring me, the anger on her face something I don't think I had ever seen before.

When she finally spoke, her voice was tight and even. "It's a lot more than that, I'm afraid."

I watched her for several moments, not believing that she could be getting so upset over such a small amount of money. Finally she nodded toward the cash register, and I followed her gaze.

It had been there for a very long time. A white copy of a sales receipt that had been taped to the side of the cash register. I'd glanced at it many times but had never known its significance or why it was there. Receipt number twenty-three fourteen. Now I reached out and carefully pulled it down as I studied the writing.

RC Plat F.D. — $2100.00.

"Twenty-one hundred dollars?" My voice was high. What in the hell did all this mean?

"Exactly." Annie's voice was heavy as she took the receipt and laid it next to the yellow copy on the counter. Except for the amount they were identical — almost. Annie was shaking her head.

"Annie." I felt suddenly very far away from her. "What's going on? What does all of this mean?" My concern was growing.

"It's a long story." She looked defeated, all brightness vacant from her features. "Awhile ago," she began, then corrected herself. "February twelfth to be exact, my ex-husband came roaring in here saying that he had found someone who was looking for a replica of a Royal Copenhagen platter. Flora Danica, to be exact. Apparently he had noticed that I had one here and said he was doing this guy a favor and picking it up for him." She stopped and shook her head. "I should have known better."

I continued to stare at her, not understanding.

"He made a big deal about filling out a receipt and entering it into the ledger, and I just wanted him to get the hell out, so I told him to leave. He had never left any money, and I never bothered to make up the thirty-eight dollars."

Her husband was a prick. I'd already figured that out. Beyond that, I didn't really understand what all this meant. Now she was shaking her head again as she stared at the receipts. Her smile was sour as she looked at me again.

"See the difference here?" She pointed to the receipts. On the store copy, it says REPL, which stands for replica. "On the original, there's no such notation."

I saw the difference between the two, but still had no idea what she was so upset about. I stared at her dumbly.

"A gentleman returned the platter about a month ago. He said that my husband had represented it as an original Royal Copenhagen. He'd thought he was getting a bargain for only twenty-one hundred dollars."

The light was beginning to go off in my head.

"Your husband sold a replica as an original?"

"Exactly." She dropped her hands to the counter. "And he pocketed over two thousand dollars in the deal. Two thousand dollars that *I* had to come up with to reimburse the guy that he sold it to."

"But you weren't the one that sold it to him!" I was livid.

"No. But the receipt that he had has Treasured Past's logo on it. He thought he was making a purchase from a reputable dealer. I had to pay him to keep my reputation."

I was shocked. What kind of a son of a bitch would do such a thing? "Annie, we have to do something to get your money back."

She was shaking her head.

"We can file suit."

She was waving me aside.

"Annie," I pleaded, my voice rising. "I'm a lawyer. Let me go after this guy."

"I have a lawyer, Kate."

"But I . . ."

"How would it look to have my lover represent me against my ex-husband? Now that would go over well." She sounded unreasonable.

"But, Annie, this isn't about us. It's about theft and —"

"I have a lawyer, Kate." She practically screamed the words, stopping me in my tracks.

"Okay, Annie. I'm sorry," I said quietly. "I was just trying to help."

"I know." She sighed and closed her eyes. "I'm sorry I raised my voice. I'm just so frustrated."

I didn't know what to say. I wanted so much to put a plan into action. My logical mind was already scripting the suit that we should file. But it was painfully obvious that she didn't want my help in the matter. I couldn't understand why. Why would she be protecting him like this?

110

The sadness in her eyes made me forget my own questions. Without another word, I circled the counter and held my arms open. She had never held me tighter.

Chapter 16

"Tonight was wonderful." Annie murmured the words against my ear as she snuggled deeper against my neck.

"I'm glad you enjoyed it," I told her while reaching up to smooth her hair.

"Beth is so sweet. Do you think she had fun?" Annie raised her head just enough so that our eyes could meet.

"I know she did," I told her. We had invited Beth and her son over for a barbeque, using the excuse that we wanted her to see what we had done to the great room. Beth had no idea that we were really celebrating her birthday. And if she *had* been suspicious, she never let on.

It felt good to have Beth and Annie in the same room, even though they'd teased me mercilessly about everything and anything imaginable. Privately, Beth had pulled me aside to tell me how happy she was that Annie and I had gotten together.

"The two of you are wonderful together, Kate."

"Do you think so?" I'd asked, suddenly insecure.

"Absolutely," she'd insisted. "Everything that I've seen tonight tells me that the two of you are so happy together. The way you laugh and interact. You're both so attentive to each other." She grinned and rolled her eyes. "It's a little sickening, actually, the way you two moon over each other."

I slapped her arm playfully.

"We don't moon," I insisted.

"Yes you do. You *both* do. But it's very sweet."

I tried to muster up a snarl but failed. Beth's face sobered.

"It's good to see you happy like this, Kate. And it's quite obvious that Annie cares for you."

Now I smiled as I remembered Beth's words.

"Beth said that it's obvious that you care for me," I told Annie. She was busily twining her fingers through mine.

"She thinks so, eh?"

I couldn't see her eyes, but could tell by the sound of her voice that she was feeling lighthearted.

"That's what she said," I told her.

"Hm." Annie pulled away again to look into my

eyes. "And what do you think? Do you think it's obvious that I care for you?" She studied my face while her fingers continued their dance with mine.

Her question made me nervous. "I can only hope that you do," was my reply.

She seemed surprised by my response. "It's not obvious to you?"

I suddenly felt shy. "Well," I began, searching for the right words. "We never really talk about us, do we? It seems like we're always so busy *doing* things together that we never really get many quiet moments like this." I watched for her reaction, but her face was carefully blank. "Don't get me wrong, Annie. I love the time that we spend together. But you must admit that we keep very busy."

Her smile was slow. "Life does seem rather full these days, doesn't it?"

"It certainly does," I agreed. "But I wouldn't change it for anything."

"Really?" Her eyes were twinkling. "There's nothing you would change if you could?"

"That's not quite true," I admitted. "For one thing, I would change my job. Although I'm not quite certain what I'd like to do, exactly."

"Uh-huh," Annie was urging me to continue to talk. "What else?"

I searched her eyes, afraid to say what I was really thinking. "The truth?"

"Of course," she encouraged me, giving my hand a squeeze and draping one leg over mine as we sat together on the couch.

My hesitation was brief.

"I would make more room for quiet time with you like this. So that we could talk more and learn more about each other. I've seen you nearly every day for months now, and I still know so little about you."

Her smile was soft. "And what would you like to know?" She leaned forward enough to drop a kiss on my chin.

"Everything." I let out a long sigh. "Your favorite color. What you were like as a child. I'd like to hear about your parents and family. I don't even know if you have any sisters or brothers."

"No siblings, unfortunately," she told me. "I think I missed not having someone to play with. Although my parents were quite wonderful." Her voice was soft and matter-of-fact. "And blue."

"Excuse me?" I'd completely lost the thread of the conversation.

"My favorite color. Blue."

"Oh." I laughed and reached out to lay my free hand on her thigh before growing more serious. I knew that I was about to enter touchy ground. "I also wonder about your marriage," I said softly. "I know you don't like to talk about it, but I'm sure that it must have been an important part of your life." I watched her closely, awaiting her reaction. I expected her to avoid the topic, and was surprised when she began to open up.

"You're right. I don't like to talk about it." She wrinkled her nose. "I don't even like to *think* about it." She closed her eyes briefly and shook herself. "It's all a bad, bad memory. In many ways it doesn't even seem real anymore. My life is so good now, and I just want to keep all that in my past. Does that make sense?"

I nodded. "He didn't hurt you, did he?"

She shook her head. "No, not physically at least.

He was just very manipulative, and I put up with it far longer than I should have."

She was curling and uncurling her fingers around mine. Then she grinned and raised an eyebrow. "In any case, why should we waste time talking about him when there are so many more interesting things to discuss."

"About your past, you mean?" I teased.

Her voice matched my playful tone. "Maybe," she shrugged.

"Ooh. Now you've got my curiosity going. What kind of skeletons are you hiding?"

Her laugh was throaty. "I'm afraid my life has probably been pretty dull. Especially compared to yours."

"What's that supposed to mean?" I feigned offense.

"Are you kidding? A young, dashing attorney like yourself? You must have devastated a number of hearts along the way."

"I don't think so," I confessed. "I've really only had one or two serious involvements. For the most part I've put my work first. Now I know that it was a mistake to do that."

"So you're a wiser woman now?"

I shrugged. "I like to think so. At least I think I have my priorities in the right place now."

Annie was nodding silently. "It sounds like I met you at just the right time."

"I think you're probably right about that."

She nodded again. "Do you want to tell me what's going on with you and work? I know you're not happy there."

"I'm not," I sighed. "But I'm in no hurry to get out. I have to change my situation, but I'm not certain what to do." I shrugged. "I'm not that worried about it. Besides, I thought we were talking about you."

She yawned and stretched her body, her arms brushing against me as she stretched. "I'm too afraid that if I tell you all my secrets that you'll lose interest in me."

"Never," I assured her.

"Besides" — her voice took on a seductive sweetness — "if we talk about everything now then eventually you'll get bored with me. Don't we have to save something to keep all the fires burning for when we're old and gray and sitting in our rockers on the front porch?"

She was probably teasing, but I wanted to take her words seriously. "Is that a proposal?" I asked.

Her smile was soft. "Maybe. Except that we've only been seeing each other for a few months and I have a firm policy about marrying someone without at least knowing them for a year first."

I almost laughed, except that I knew she was partially serious. I sighed heavily. "You're so sensible, Annie Walsh."

"I try to be, Katherine Brennan." She took my hand and lifted it to her mouth, pressing her lips to my fingertips. "But I do admit that I have entertained a number of fantasies that include you."

"Really?" Now my curiosity was definitely piqued. "Like what?"

"Besides the obvious?" She bounced her eyebrows mischievously. Then she took a deep breath and spoke quietly. "I fantasize what it would be like to wake up next to you every day. To share a home with you and maybe remodel the whole thing from top to bottom."

117

I was having trouble holding back my smile. My heart was singing as I listened to her words. I kissed her fingers now, urging her to continue. "I think how wonderful my life has become since meeting you, and I can't help but think that I'd really enjoy growing old with you, Kate."

I couldn't hold back the smile any longer. She had spoken so eloquently what I myself had been thinking. I could only think about the future and pray that nothing would get in our way.

"You look awfully serious." She tipped her head. "I hope I didn't just say the wrong thing. I wouldn't want to scare you away."

I rushed to reassure her. "You can't scare me away, Annie." I realized how much I loved saying her name. Our eyes locked and our expressions both wavered between happiness and caution.

My breath rattled as I pushed a sigh from my lungs.

"You know that I think I love you, don't you?" It was such a silly way to say the words, but I couldn't hold them back any longer.

"I had certainly hoped so." She smiled lazily and lifted both arms to wrap around my neck. "Because I think I probably love you too."

I would have grinned, except that her mouth had found mine and she was nibbling on my bottom lip and causing the most curious shivers to trickle up and down my spine.

Chapter 17

I was dreading my meeting with Melanie. After all, there was nothing really to say, and there was certainly no chance of reaching any kind of settlement that Donald Junior would agree to. The whole nightmare was going to end up in front of a judge, and Melanie's client was going to get screwed. As much as I wanted to turn the tables on my boss's son, I knew that I was powerless to do so. I had absolutely no ammunition to fire.

Melanie's office was part of the Cambridge Family Law Center on Massachusetts Avenue. Sitting in the cramped space that I had once shared, I compared my surroundings with the lush elegance that I'd grown accustomed to. The difference was unmistakable, but being in Melanie's office reminded of the practice that I'd left behind. Maybe it was time to reconsider and go back to my old practice after all.

"So tell me that you have some good news, Kate." Melanie was all business.

"I honestly wish I did, Melanie. But I have nothing new to offer."

Her lips were drawn in a straight line. "So we go to court," she stated evenly. "I was hoping to avoid that."

I nodded in full agreement. "I know, Melanie. I want you to know that I tried reasoning with Gold and his father, but they just won't budge."

"He's a real bastard, Kate."

"I know that. Maybe even better than you do." I paused, contemplating just how much I should say. To hell with it, I decided. I had no real loyalty to Donald Junior.

"Listen, Melanie. For what it's worth, I think you should know that I brought up everything you told me with both of them. I told them that it could get really ugly in court and that there was no doubt in my mind that you would be raising all the issues about the house being inherited by your client. I also mentioned the fact that they hadn't even lived together for four years. I told his father that I didn't think that any of this would bode well in front of a judge."

"And?"

"Between you and me, he practically laughed at me and reminded me that he had an awful lot of friends on the bench and that there wasn't one of them that didn't owe him a favor." I bit off each word bitterly.

Melanie whistled low. "So they're not going to pull any punches."

I shook my head. "Not at all. They welcome the chance to get in front of a judge."

Melanie was shaking her head. "This sucks, Kate."

I had to agree. "I know it does. Believe me, I've tried to figure out how to get around this mess, but I don't see any way out for your client."

She looked genuinely saddened.

"I'm sorry, Melanie."

"I know, Kate. Me too." She sighed. "This is going to be awful." Tired eyes fell to mine. "Any other good news for me?"

"None. I'm sorry." I couldn't believe how awful I was feeling. *So much for not having any emotional involvement with my cases.* Instead of feeling bad for my clients, I now found myself in the position of feeling guilty about the clients my firm now represented. Whether it was representing Donald Junior in his divorce case or representing a corporate conglomerate doing a takeover of a small business, all I felt now was guilt and sadness toward the people who stood in my firm's way.

"All right." Melanie sighed and pushed herself away from the desk. "So I guess this means I'll see you a week from tomorrow, right?"

I didn't bother trying to hide my groan. "I'm afraid so." I stood and lifted my briefcase, noting that she didn't bother to rise with me. She looked so defeated as she sat behind her desk, staring out the window, already forgetting I was there.

" 'Bye, Melanie."

She mumbled a good-bye, and I decided there was nothing I could do except leave her to her thoughts.

I was so distracted when I closed the door to Melanie's office that I barely noticed her. She was sitting just six feet away, wearing one of her favorite cotton dresses, hair pulled back from her shoulders. Even after I noticed her, it took several long moments for my mind to register her image and recognize her. It was so out of context to see her outside of our normal routine.

"Annie?"

Her eyes lit up, then just as quickly they clouded over as a quizzical look fell over her features.

"Hi." She jumped to her feet. "What are you doing here?" she asked.

I grimaced. "Business. Painful business at that."

"I didn't realize that you knew Melanie." It took me a moment to see her nervousness, and I began to wonder why she would be sitting in the Cambridge Family Law Center. Then I remembered the trouble she'd had with her ex-husband, and I relaxed.

My smile was reassuring. "I've known Melanie for years, actually. We used to work here together a lot before . . ."

The door that I had just closed to Melanie's office suddenly flew open, and the look on Melanie's face was something close to horror.

"Are you okay?" Annie and I said the words at nearly the same instant, watching while Melanie looked first at Annie and then back at me.

"You two know each other?" Her eyes continued to shift between us.

I laughed. "Very well, actually." I turned toward

my lover and felt my stomach begin to turn as I saw the look on her face. Her complexion had paled, and she looked like someone who was in shock. She was staring directly at Melanie. I followed her gaze and saw that Melanie was returning the stare. Something was definitely wrong. It felt as though I had just stumbled into a room and caught my lover having an affair. My mind reeled as I glanced quickly between them.

"What's going on?" I demanded. "Why are you two acting this way?"

I heard Annie let out a huge sigh beside me. Melanie seemed to recover from whatever it was that had gotten her so upset, and a sort of calmness fell over her.

"I think we have a problem," she said quietly.

I felt completely disjointed. "With what?" I asked stupidly.

Melanie kept her attention focused on Annie. "Annie, Kate is representing your husband in your divorce case."

"Excuse me?" Obviously, I hadn't heard her correctly.

"You're *representing* him?" The sound of her voice was like a screech in my ear. I felt incoherent, as if everything was suddenly happening in slow motion and I couldn't quite keep up. This was just plain ludicrous.

"You mean Donald Gold?" My eyes swam to Melanie and back to Annie.

Annie was seething. "Of course I mean Donald Gold. You're his *lawyer*?"

"Well, yes. But I don't understand, Annie. What's this all about?" My eyes flew back to Melanie's, begging for her to help me make sense of the confusion.

"This is all some kind of setup, isn't it?" Annie began rambling irrationally. "He put you up to this, didn't he." She began to move across the floor, pacing.

"Annie." I said her name several times, but it was as if she wasn't hearing me. Then she stopped pacing, her face inches from mine. Her lips curled sarcastically.

"You're good," she laughed. "I fell for it completely." She shook her head, anger and sadness mixing together in her eyes. "Make sure you tell Donald that whatever he was paying, he certainly got his money's worth this time." She turned and began walking away from me.

"Annie." I called after her and took two steps in her direction when I felt Melanie's hand clamp down firmly on my shoulder. I tried to shake her off.

"Annie!" I knew my voice was too loud, but I didn't care. People were staring at me from all corners of the office. Annie didn't bother waiting for an elevator. She threw open the door to the staircase and disappeared from my sight.

"Come into my office." I could barely hear Melanie speaking the words close to my ear.

I turned on her, furious and bewildered. "No!" I pulled my arm from her grasp. "What in the hell is going on, Mel?"

Her expression was grim as she grabbed my arm and pulled me into her office. I followed her in a stupefied trance, dropping in the chair in front of her desk while she closed the door behind her.

"Jesus Christ," she muttered. "What a mess." She dropped into her chair and rubbed her eyes. "Why didn't you tell me that you knew her?" She lifted accusing eyes to mine.

"Melanie." My temper was almost out of control. "I don't even know what the fuck is going on here. All I know is that my lover is suddenly furious with me and now you're accusing me of something that I know nothing about." I shifted forward in my chair. "What is she talking about, Mel? What's going on?"

"You really didn't know?"

"Know *what*?" I could have strangled her.

She stared at me, eyes flat. "Annie is Donald Gold's wife."

I stared at her. Not quite comprehending. Not quite understanding. Definitely not believing.

"That's ridiculous," I insisted. Annie was divorced, wasn't she? Didn't she say that she *used to be* married? Didn't she refer to her husband as her *ex?*

"It's true, Kate."

I refused to believe her. "That's impossible. Donald Junior is married to someone named Hildegard Gold. I reviewed the divorce papers, Mel." My voice was heavy with sarcasm.

Melanie nodded, her voice quiet now. "Annie's name is Hildegard Ann Gold."

"No," I insisted. "It's Annie Walsh."

Melanie took a deep breath. "Walsh is her maiden name. She kept using it because it made things easier for business purposes. Her parents owned Treasured Past and it just made sense to continue using the name that everyone was familiar with."

I blinked hard and began to panic. *This can't be true. It can't.* But my stomach was sinking and my legs felt weak.

"Jesus Christ." My stomach began to churn, and I

leaned forward, stars snapping and popping behind my closed eyes.

"You had no idea?" Melanie prompted.

"No," I insisted. "Why would I have any reason to think that Annie was Gold's wife? She told me that she was divorced." I thought about it for a moment. "At least I thought that's what she said." I shook my head, trying to clear the cobwebs.

"How long have you been seeing each other?" Her voice was quiet and steady.

"A few months." I shook my head, trying to sift through it all. "We never discussed her husband. She always seemed to avoid the topic." I stared at my hands, then at Melanie. "Why would she have kept that from me?" I asked, hurt beginning to replace the anger.

Melanie shrugged. "I'm not sure, Kate. Unless it was because she knew she was almost divorced and she didn't want it to be part of your relationship."

I kept shaking my head, not believing it. "This can't be happening," I said aloud. Then I turned back to Melanie. "This is a nightmare."

Melanie was nodding. "In more ways than one, Kate," she began. "I know you're upset and that you're questioning your relationship right now," she paused. "But just think for a moment about the implications on the court case, Kate."

She had my full attention now. I didn't think I could take much more. I needed to go after Annie, to talk to her and try to figure out what had happened.

"Did Gold's father have any idea that you knew Annie?" Melanie was shifting into attorney mode.

"Of course not. He doesn't know anything about

my personal life." As soon as I said the words, I wasn't so sure any more.

"Are you sure? Is it possible that he set you up somehow?" Melanie's eyes were driving into mine.

I tried to think back and remember the timing of everything. "I can't be certain," I admitted. "I can't imagine that he would have any knowledge of my relationship with Annie. But then again, I wouldn't put it past him to manipulate something if he thought it would get him what he wanted."

Melanie chewed on this thought for several moments. "So it's possible," she began, "that Gold gave you this case knowing that you were involved with his son's wife."

My blood was beginning to boil as I joined her train of thought. My fists were clenching as she continued.

"It's possible that he knew that sooner or later you would figure out who Annie was and that the entire case would blow up in our faces."

"And if Gold's main argument is that he found his wife having sex with another woman . . ."

"Imagine what kind of ammunition he would have if he somehow managed to twist all this in front of a judge and make it appear as though Annie seduced you in order to compromise your position with your client."

My head hurt. "This is crazy." I rubbed my eyes, my mind drifting to Annie. Where would she have gone?

"Maybe." Melanie shrugged. "Maybe not." She leaned forward. "We need to tread carefully, Kate. We need to step back and plan our next moves."

I knew she was right, but I was beyond reasoning. "I know," I sighed. "We both need some time to think. I need to talk to Annie . . ."

Melanie was quiet for several moments. "Then go and talk to her, Kate. See what you can do and what you can find out."

I was already on my feet.

"But keep me posted, okay? Promise me we'll put our heads together and come up with something."

"Okay." I reached for my briefcase. "I'll be in touch."

"And Kate?"

I turned back to face her as I opened the door. "Yeah?"

Her smile was weak. "Good luck, Kate. Annie's a sweetheart, and she's been through an awful lot. Just remember that, okay?"

I nodded, digesting her words.

"Thanks," I stammered, feeling my throat beginning to constrict. "She means everything to me, Mel." I tried to smile. "Everything."

Chapter 18

My instinct was to drive to Treasured Past. It was Tuesday, and so I knew that the store was supposed to open. My car came to a screeching halt directly in front of the building. The CLOSED sign hung in the window, and I checked my watch. Almost one o'clock. The store was supposed to open at noon.

Refusing to give up so easily, I threw open the car door and ran to the front door. The doorknob wouldn't budge.

"Dammit." I had the key to the store on my key chain, and I held it in my hand, staring at it and turning it over several times. Somehow using the key to get into Annie's store felt wrong under the circumstances. The way she had left Melanie's office, it was impossible for me to predict how she might react if she found me waiting for her inside her own store. She would feel threatened, no doubt. I managed the few steps back to my car and slid in behind the steering wheel.

There had to be a solution, a way to find her.

"Well, duh!" I said out loud. I could just go to her house. I placed the key in the ignition and then dropped my hand, a cold finger curling up my spine. *I've never even been to her house. I don't even know where she lives!*

I fell back against the seat, mouth agape and dejection flooding over me. "Who's been manipulating who, Annie?" Again I spoke out loud. Things suddenly began to fall into place.

Annie had always been resistant to talking about herself. She avoided talking about her ex-husband and virtually anything else about her past or personal life. She had never even once invited me to her house. At the time I hadn't given it a second thought. I'd been too happy to have her in my home day in and out. It had certainly crossed my mind a few times that she seemed unusually reluctant to share some parts of her life with me, but I had overlooked all the warning signs.

"You lied to me."

She *had* told me that she was no longer married. I was certain of it now.

I contemplated going back to my office but dismissed it immediately. Then I remembered the papers in my briefcase, divorce papers that included the address of the home that Donald Gold wanted to take from his wife. *His wife!*

I could go there now, I thought. I could confront her and demand to know why she lied to me. My mind began to run through various scenarios, none of them playing out well.

Shutting my eyes, I tried to sort through everything that had happened.

What if Melanie was right? What if Donald Gold had somehow set me up to represent his son because he knew that I was seeing Annie? I didn't know how he could have found out, but I certainly knew it was possible.

The image of Annie happily married to Donald Junior swam into my mind. I still couldn't believe it and shook my head, forcing the image away.

Why had Annie lied to me? Had she known more about my association with Donald's father than I realized? Surely she must have known that I worked for Brown, Benning, and Gold. We rarely talked about my work, but there had certainly been dozens of my business cards strewn about the house. My imagination took some creative twists and turns.

Maybe I *had* been set up, but maybe it had been Annie that had been manipulating me. Had she found out that I worked for Donald's father before we'd started seeing each other? Was it possible that she had seen an opportunity to short-circuit her husband's demands by ingratiating herself with me?

I allowed my thoughts to drift along these lines. If Annie had believed that she could make me fall for her, then maybe she had planned it all along. As her lover, wouldn't I do everything in my power to dissuade Donald from going after their home?

I raised one hand and rubbed my eyes. It was beginning to make too much sense. Was it possible that she could be that shrewd? That cold and calculating?

I let out a long whistle while the thought settled over me.

But wouldn't she recognize the legal obstacles in her way? I should be withdrawing from the case right now, I reasoned. If our relationship came out, Donald would pull me from the case immediately.

Or would he? Maybe it was Donald who had plans for hanging me out to dry.

I was too confused, too uncertain to try to sort it all out. Trying to push my thoughts aside, I revved the engine and slid the car into gear. I couldn't get home fast enough.

Chapter 19

Three days without seeing Annie. Not a single phone call. Not one. I'd left messages at her home and at the shop every day, telling her that she was completely wrong about what she suspected and begging her to call me. But my phone never rang.

Each day I arrived home from work, hoping and praying that she would be in the great room, inspecting whatever work had been completed that day. Each day I was disappointed.

Disappointed was an understatement. *Devastated* was probably closer to the truth. I stood in the center of the room now. The first Friday evening in months that I wasn't going to spend with her. The ache in my heart seemed to radiate throughout my body as sadness and frustration overwhelmed me.

The smell of sawdust hung in the air. They'd finished sanding all the woodwork. The white paint had been completely stripped from the stone chimney. It wouldn't take long for the workers to finish staining and sealing and applying all the finishing touches.

And for what? Tears of frustration were threatening as I allowed myself to feel pity. It was true enough that I'd wanted to do something with this room. But it had been Annie's enthusiasm that had propelled me to have the work done. The sheer thrill and excitement on Annie's face had been the motivation for me. And now I knew that I could never walk into this room without thinking of her.

I had spent countless hours trying to decide whether or not to show up on her doorstep. I'd driven by Treasured Past at least once each day, only to find the CLOSED sign propped up in the window.

The phone began to ring and I rushed back to the living room, my heart hopeful as I reached for the phone.

"Hello?"

"Kate?"

My heart sank. "Melanie?" I collapsed on the couch and listened to several moments of silence.

"She fired me, Kate."

"What?" Could things possibly get any worse?

"Just now." Mel's voice sounded hollow. "I received a call from her new attorney, informing me that my services would no longer be needed."

"Shit, Mel. Did she give you a reason?"

"He," she corrected me. "Bob Gleason has the case now." Bob was another old associate that Melanie and I had both worked with or against on many occasions.

"What did he say?"

"That he'd been reluctant to take the case and that he made it plain to Annie that he was dead against what she was doing. But she made it clear to him that she didn't want me representing her." I could hear the sadness in her voice. "Apparently Annie told him that she had concerns that the two of us were conspiring against her."

"That's ridiculous!" I shouted. "When did she get so paranoid?"

She sighed. "I'm not surprised, really. You have no idea what that man and his family have put her through. She's convinced that she'll never get out from under them, and this just plays into her worst fears."

"But, Melanie, I had no idea about any of this."

"I know. But there's nothing I can do about it anymore." She hesitated for a moment before continuing. "You should probably know that they plan on petitioning the court, on the grounds that the Golds conspired against her, and that you and I went along with it."

I felt like the wind had been knocked out of me. I began nibbling on my bottom lip, my mind going in circles.

"That's the worst thing she could do."

"I know, Kate. I'm not sure if it's a stall tactic or if she really thinks they can present a case."

"I need to get her to talk to me, Mel." Plans began to formulate in my mind. "You have to get hold of Bob. Let him know that he has to convince Annie to hold off on the petition."

"And how am I going to convince either of them to do that?"

"I don't know, Mel. And technically we aren't having this conversation."

We were both silent for several moments.

"What do you have in mind, Kate?"

"I'm not even sure," I admitted. "But you have to convince Bob to give me until Tuesday before he files that petition."

"That's the court date."

"I know that. But if they're going to file, it won't hurt if it's at the last minute." I had to talk to Annie and convince her that she was completely off base about everything. "Do it, Mel. Call him. Buy me some time."

"I'll try." Her voice sounded resigned.

"Try hard, Mel."

"What are you plotting over there, Kate? I can practically hear the wheels in your head spinning."

For the first time in days, I actually laughed. "I'm not even sure myself yet," I told her. "But whatever I come up with, it's probably grossly unethical and you'd be better off not knowing anything about it."

"Be careful, Kate." She sounded grim.

"I will," I assured her. "Just convince Bob to put things on hold."

We said good-bye and hung up. Annie and I were going to have a long talk, and yesterday wasn't soon enough for me.

I picked up the phone again, hesitating only briefly before punching in Annie's phone number. I slammed down the receiver when I heard the answering machine pick up.

"Fine," I muttered. "If you won't pick up the phone then you're going to have to slam the door in my face."

I ran upstairs to change into shorts and a T-shirt. Then I grabbed my keys and headed out the door.

Heading down Storrow Drive, I pulled off at the exit nearest to Treasured Past, thinking it might be at least worth another drive by. I cruised by slowly and noted that the CLOSED sign was propped in its place.

Great. I punched the accelerator and then just as quickly hit the brakes. Something wasn't quite right. I looked back at the store, trying to see past the sign in the window. The lights were on.

I checked my watch, noting that it was nearly seven-thirty. The store closed at five o'clock every day, and the lights were on a timer that went off at six o'clock. That meant that Annie must be inside.

Steering the car to the curb, I felt my heart begin to race. I didn't know what I would say to her if she *was* in there. What if she refused to listen to me? The thought of Annie rejecting me gave me a sickening feeling. But I couldn't worry about that now. Cutting the engine, I took several deep breaths to steady my nerves.

I stole a look inside as I got closer to the door. I could see no movement, but I was still certain that Annie must be here. I gingerly reached for the handle and turned it, hoping that it would turn easily. It was locked.

Now I had a real dilemma. I could knock, in which case she could either choose to ignore me or simply refuse to open the door. Or I could use my key. For a moment I wondered if she'd changed the locks, but the key slid in and turned the lock easily. My heart pounding loudly, I let myself in.

The bell above the door jingled, and I thought my heart would explode. Trying to calm my nerves, I shut the door behind me, making sure that the lock was bolted before I stepped farther inside. Listening closely for signs of life, my ears were filled with empty silence.

Goose bumps began crawling along my skin, and I suddenly felt reluctant about letting myself into the store. I knew that it wasn't technically breaking and entering. But Annie could certainly make this look bad if she wanted to.

"Annie?" I called her name softly and listened for a reply, hearing nothing. The hum of fluorescent lighting drew me farther into the room, where I heard a faint scraping sound coming from the back of the store.

As I drew closer, it sounded like someone was lifting and moving heavy furniture. I imagined that Annie must be moving some new purchase in from the loading dock outside, and I wasn't far off in my assumption.

Her back was toward me and I watched her lifting one end of a mahogany dining room table. She was walking backward and pulling the table with her, the legs scraping on the oak floor. She set the table down, and I chose that moment to interrupt her.

"Annie?" She jumped back and raised a hand to her chest when she saw me.

"You scared the hell out of me."

"I'm sorry." Seeing her only made me forget about

what had transpired over the past week. I took a step forward, palms up, and my stomach dropped when she stepped back and away from me.

"What are you doing here?" Her voice was hard, eyes accusing.

"We have to talk, Annie." I kept my voice calm and quiet.

"So you just decided to let yourself in?"

"I've been letting myself in every day for months." I fought back sarcasm. "You haven't returned any of my phone calls, and I had to talk to you before Tuesday."

"Talk to my lawyer," she snapped, turning back to the task of moving the table.

I could feel myself growing angry, and it took some effort to try to curb it.

"Don't be an ass, Annie. We have to talk." In spite of my efforts, I could hear the frustration in my voice.

"No, Kate." Her voice exploded as she faced me square on. "Technically I shouldn't be talking to you at all. You are representing my husband in a divorce case that could absolutely destroy me in more ways than one. Does your client know that you're here?"

"Of course not."

"And does he know that you've been fraternizing with the enemy for months now?" Her hands were planted on her hips. "Or was I right in assuming that he put you up to this from the very beginning."

I didn't recognize her. This was nothing like the woman that I had known and spent so much time with these past months. She was angry and completely unreasonable.

I sighed. "I'm honestly not sure exactly what the

Golds know and don't know," I told her. "But I've never discussed you in any personal way with either of them."

Her eyes fluttered over me. "I don't believe you."

My jaw dropped. "I didn't even know that Donald Gold was your husband until three days ago!"

"That's what you say. But I don't believe that either."

I wanted to scream. "Annie, you told me you were divorced. I didn't even know you were married, *remember?*"

She shrugged, her eyes closed. "That's what you led me to believe, at least. But I find it all difficult to believe now."

"Believe what?"

She had no patience. "I find it difficult to believe that you had no idea that I was married to your client. I cannot believe that you were representing him all that time and didn't figure out that he and I were married. It just wouldn't be that hard to figure out."

I shook my head. "I didn't know, Annie."

"You certainly didn't do much digging around," she snorted. "Even your father knows about Donald."

He did? I began to chide myself. Had I really fallen asleep so badly on this case? Had I been so caught up in feeling manipulated by Gold that I hadn't bothered to do my homework? I felt helpless.

"Look, Annie. You can go ahead and think that I'm a shitty lawyer. The fact is that I didn't know."

I could tell by the look on her face that I wasn't reaching her. She was steadfast in her refusal to believe me.

"Let me tell you what I think," she replied,

settling back against the table that she'd just been moving.

"I think that Donald's father put you up to everything. I think that he made it worth your while to ingratiate yourself with me and get me into your bed."

"You're being irrational, Annie."

"Am I?" She raised one brow. "He knows you're a lesbian, doesn't he?"

"We've never discussed it," I replied.

"But he knows," she assured me. "He was absolutely ballistic when he found out that his son had caught me with a woman. It would just be too perfect for him to select you to represent his son."

I couldn't disagree with her. Hadn't I suspected the same thing?

"I don't care about them, Annie. I care about us." I was beginning to plead with her.

"Do you?" Her voice was so cold. "I think it was all part of the plan. Once I became involved with you I pretty much killed any chance I had with my settlement."

"You think I faked the whole thing?" I was incredulous.

She nodded. "The evidence speaks for itself, Kate. The Golds have a lot of money and power. It's not difficult for me to believe that you've been paid quite well to bring me down."

"Bring you down?" My laugh was harsh. "You've been watching too many movies."

"And you're underestimating your employer," she replied sharply. Then she paused as if rethinking her response. "Unless I'm underestimating you right now and you're just playing me again."

She shook her head, her voice quieting.

"I don't know what I believe, Kate. But right now I can't believe a word that you're saying. We shouldn't be talking at all."

"You really don't believe me?"

She shook her head. "I can't, Kate. It would be foolish of me to do so." She sighed heavily. "He's going to take my home, Kate."

"Yeah," I snapped. "A home you never even invited me to." My anger was growing. "You went out of your way to keep your marriage and everything about your life a secret from me."

She studied me momentarily before shrugging. Her nonchalance infuriated me.

"You told me that you were divorced," I reminded her. "It was you who lied to *me*, Annie. Remember?"

She studied me for several moments more before choosing her words carefully. "You can leave any time you like, Kate. You know where the door is."

"Dammit, Annie. I can't believe you're acting this way." My emotions were somewhere between anger and tears.

"And I can't believe you would come here and try to convince me that our entire relationship wasn't anything but a farce." Her eyes were livid. "You can let your client know that he may very well end up with my parents' home, but I'm not going to just roll over and let him have it."

I remembered what Melanie had told me, that Annie and her lawyer were planning to petition the court and accuse us of conspiracy and tampering and god-only-knows what else.

"Annie, I have no idea whether the Golds have manipulated this situation. But you have to know that

I've never lied to you. I haven't conspired against you in any way."

"You're just trying to save your butt," she snapped.

"No, Annie. That's where you're wrong." I set my jaw firmly. "I'm trying to save *us*."

We stared at each other for the longest time while I wondered if there was any chance that I had gotten through to her. Something close to sadness seemed to drop over her features. But then she folded her arms across her chest, and her lips lifted in a condescending smile.

"I think it's time for you to go, Counselor. I'll see you in court."

She scored a direct hit. The anger evaporated until only the helplessness remained. Without another word, I turned and retraced my steps to the front door.

Chapter 20

Sunday was perhaps the longest day of my life. I spent most of the day with Beth, crying on her shoulder. It had taken nearly an hour just to explain everything that had happened. It sounded so unbelievable that I had a hard time believing everything that had happened myself.

Beth's response went from disbelief to anger and, finally, to sadness. Somewhere along the line she'd tried to help me to see Annie's point of view. If she had really been under the Golds' thumb for so long, then it made sense that she was now suspicious of me.

"You have no idea what she's been through, Kate," Beth reasoned.

"If I don't, it's because she didn't tell me. She never told me anything about her past. And what little she did speak about was only after a lot of prompting on my part."

Beth's face was grim.

"I'm sorry, Kate. This is a nightmare."

I could only agree with her. It *was* a nightmare. Then my mind flashed forward to the morning. At some point I would have to meet with Donald Gold. What would I tell him?

Ethically, I was bound to tell him everything. I was bound to tell him that I had just discovered that I had been in a relationship with his daughter-in-law for months. I mentioned this fact to Beth, and she tried without success at some humor.

"Then your nightmare has just begun," she informed me. As if I didn't already know that.

"Thanks for the encouragement," I told her.

"Do you *have* to tell them?" Beth asked.

"I should." I paused, thinking it over. "I have information that could impact my client's case. Besides, they may already know about it."

"Do you honestly think that they would set you up like that?"

I shrugged. "They might. In which case they're either waiting for me to come forward or are planning to spring the information on me or the court at the last minute. I'm sure they would use the information to their greatest advantage."

"It doesn't sound like you can possibly win this, Kate."

My laugh was full of irony. "Unfortunately, it looks

like I could very well win the court case. Especially if Gold calls in his favors." My thoughts drifted to Annie. I had felt badly for Donald Junior's wife when I didn't even know who she was. Now that I knew it was Annie, my heart was beyond heavy with regret.

"But you'll lose Annie," Beth reminded me.

"I probably already have," I told her. "She was so angry, Beth. I didn't even recognize her."

"She thinks you betrayed her, Kate." Her words were doing little to soothe me.

"I know, Beth. And I don't think I stand a chance in hell of convincing her otherwise."

I don't know if I slept at all that night. My mind was running on fast forward, jumping from one thought to another. Time after time, I replayed my conversation with Annie. Then my thoughts would skitter forward to my meeting with Donald Gold in the morning.

No matter how the conversation played out in my mind, I always ended up feeling worse than I had from the previous scenario. I would either get fired, stripped of my license or, worse yet, Donald Gold would grin at me and pat me on the back. But no matter what Donald's reaction, or how the judge would rule, one thing was certain. There was no way I could win this with Annie.

I held the pillow that had cradled her head so many nights close to my chest, hugging it tightly. At some point during the night an important thought crossed my mind, one that I told myself to hang on to. When the alarm went off at six-thirty, I awoke with a nagging feeling. I was supposed to remember something. Something important that might just be the way out of this mess. Had I been dreaming?

No, I didn't think so. But it wasn't until after I'd showered and dressed and was heading out the door that I remembered what it was. As I mulled over the idea, a small smile came to my lips. *This might work*, I told myself. *This may just be the solution.*

The first thing I did when I arrived at the office was pick up the phone and dial Melanie's number.

"Have you heard anything?" I didn't even bother to greet her.

"I'm not exactly in the loop anymore, remember?" From the tone of her voice, I could tell that Melanie hadn't gotten much sleep over the weekend either.

"I know. I was just wondering whether or not you've spoken with Bob." As tired as I was, both my mind and heart were racing.

"I did. He was very reluctant," Mel sighed.

My heart sank. "So he's not going to hold off filing the petition?"

"He didn't say that he wouldn't."

I felt hope rise. If I just had enough time . . . "But he didn't say he would, either, did he?"

"No." Her voice picked up. "But you know how it is, Counselor. All that double-speak and spouting about attorney-client privilege and ethics. Then of course he mentioned how sometimes papers get filed but somehow get misplaced until it's too late in the day to do anything about it."

I almost laughed. Bob would do everything he could to hold off filing the petition and give me a chance to make things right. I had bought a little time. I glanced at my watch. Eight hours to be exact.

"Thanks for trying, Mel. I appreciate it."

"Whatever I can do, Kate. You know that." She hesitated briefly. "So do you have a plan in mind?"

I did, and I had something that I wanted to ask her. But paranoia began to grip me. I had to choose my words carefully.

"I do, actually." I told her. "And I have one question for you."

She didn't respond, so I went ahead and asked, trying to be as vague as possible. "Is there any other information that your client gave you recently about her husband? Anything that might be of value?"

"I'm afraid not. At least nothing more than what I've already shared with you."

My jaw began to work. It didn't make sense, really. But just because Annie had decided against using the information, it didn't mean that I had to do the same.

"Thanks, Melanie." I was hopeful again. "I'll be in touch."

"Before the end of the day?"

I laughed. "Maybe. We'll see how things go. I imagine that we'll chat sometime before nightfall."

Melanie sounded almost relieved. "Good luck, Kate. I'll talk to you later."

I said good-bye and began scripting a conversation with Donald in my mind. It may have been foolish on my part, but a sick little part of me was actually looking forward to our conversation.

I decided not to wait any longer. If everything went as I hoped, then time was absolutely crucial. Steadying my nerves, I left my office and headed down the hall. Better to catch him off guard and in his own office, I decided. The dynamics would at least give me the illusion of control, and I needed all the help I could get.

I could hear him growling at someone from several offices away. Millicent was standing guard, and she held me at bay while he continued his tirade. He was on the phone, ripping into some poor fool.

I explained to Millie that I needed to speak to him immediately. "It has to do with his son's divorce case." I dropped my voice down conspiratorially, and her interest seemed to pick right up.

She lowered her voice as well, assuring me she would see what she could do before disappearing into Donald's office. I could hear him pontificating at length before he finally paused and gave his attention to his secretary. Two sentences later, he was slamming down the phone and calling out to me to enter his office.

Here we go. I took several deep breaths. *No turning back now.*

He was all smiles when I entered the room, waving me inside and actually standing as I approached his desk.

"Sit down, Kate." His voice boomed. "Are we ready for the big day tomorrow?"

"I believe we are, sir." I spoke confidently.

"Good, good. We'll all be glad when the whole ordeal is over."

"Yes sir." I held my tongue and watched him closely, looking for some sign that he knew more than he was telling me.

He was watching me in return, eyes narrowing as he frowned.

"Is there something else, then? Something else that you wanted to discuss?"

I spoke cautiously, dropping my voice for his ears only. "There is something else, sir. Something that I'm not quite sure how to handle."

"What's this about?"

"Your son's case, sir."

He was frowning again. I recalled our last conversation about his son's divorce and how he had belittled my concerns. No doubt he was gearing up for another tongue-lashing.

He was barely containing his impatience. "Yes, Kate. What is it? Speak up."

I took another deep breath and let it out slowly. If Donald Gold had set me up the way Annie imagined he had, I would certainly know it shortly.

"I was recently made aware of some information about your son, sir," I paused, watching his reaction closely. "Since he is my client, I thought that I should speak to him directly. But given the nature of the information and my relationship with you and the firm, I thought it might be more appropriate to bring it to you."

He was frowning again. I wasn't quite sure how to interpret his slow reaction. But knowing what I did about Donald Junior, I imagined that this wasn't the first time that someone had approached his father with information that wasn't exactly flattering.

"Does this information have any impact on the proceedings tomorrow?"

"I'm afraid that it might," I told him, carefully keeping my voice even.

He finally sat down, pulling himself close to his desk as he leaned forward, hands folded loosely.

When he didn't speak, I decided to rephrase what I had said. "As I said, my first instinct was to discuss this directly with your son. But I wasn't sure if I should come to you first."

He was nibbling on his bottom lip. "You mean you didn't know whether or not you should cover your ass." His voice was no longer friendly.

I smiled briefly and nodded my head. "Something like that, sir." Better to play the game his way.

"Then you probably did the right thing in coming to me first. What is it then? What has my son done this time?"

For a moment I almost felt sorry for him. From the tone of his voice, I imagined that he had spent a lifetime having conversations that began just like this one.

I cleared my throat to steady myself and launched into the speech that I'd been scripting in my mind.

"I've been made aware of some information that could prove quite damaging to your son." Here is where I had to choose my words very carefully. "Apparently on at least two occasions, your son has sold merchandise to people using the name and receipts of his wife's antique store."

Donald continued to stare at me, displaying patience for the first time in my presence.

"The problem is that your son represented these

items as genuine antiques, when in fact they were just reproductions."

He was instantly relieved, dismissing my concerns easily.

"That doesn't sound like a problem to me," he said. "He made a mistake."

"That would be true, sir, except there are additional details that you should know about."

He frowned again, clamping his mouth shut.

"In one instance, the item was in the store, marked and priced as a replica. Your son removed it from the store and sold it to buyers that he had found through other avenues. Apparently your son represented and sold the piece as an original, and pocketed the money from each sale."

The crease between Donald's brows deepened, and for the very first time, I felt like I might actually have the upper hand.

"In the other situation," I continued, "the merchandise didn't come from the shop at all. But your son produced a receipt with the store's name on it, apparently to give the item a look of authenticity."

"Is there more?" he growled, no longer so quick to dismiss me and my concerns.

"Yes sir. In both cases he doctored the books at the store. Entries and receipts are all in his handwriting. Both of the buyers have also returned the items to the store, and your son's wife has produced refunds for the inflated price that each paid." I paused, drawing out my summation. "There is a solid paper trail, sir. And witnesses."

There. I'd planted the seed. Now I just had to make sure that I didn't say too much, and that I let Donald Senior take the direction that would cause himself and his family to save as much face as possible.

His reaction was interesting to watch. He made no blind denials or insistence that his son would never do such a thing. I could only imagine the number of times that Donald had bailed his son out from one disaster or another.

"How do you know they're not just blowing smoke?" His voice was unusually calm and quiet.

"I actually saw the evidence, Donald." I experienced a small pleasure as I changed my posture. I was no longer just an employee. Now I would play the comforting friend and confidant as well.

"How did you manage that?" he asked quickly.

I dropped my voice and confided in him. "It probably wasn't very ethical on my part, if you know what I mean. But it had to do with your son and the firm, so . . ." I let the sentence trail off, leading him to believe whatever he wanted to.

He offered a small smile. "I appreciate your loyalty and whatever risks you might have taken in getting your hands on this information."

Relief spread over me. He'd swallowed the hook. I waited quietly for his next words. If he knew anything about my relationship with Annie, now would be the time for him to confront me. I held my breath and waited.

"Do you think they'll use this information?" It was a ridiculous question, of course.

I looked at him evenly, again thinking carefully before I responded. "Wouldn't you?"

His smile was ironic as he nodded, his voice quiet and thoughtful. "And of course they wouldn't let us know in advance that they had this information. I expect that it was their plan to spring this on us once we were in court." I could almost see the chess game that he played in his mind. "Smart move on their part, not to tip their hand."

I nodded. There was no point in replying.

"Is there anything else I should be aware of?" He was back to business.

"I think that's it, Donald. I just need some direction from you at this point. Shall I contact your son and pass along this information?" I knew there was no chance in hell that he would let me talk to Donald Junior.

"Oh no." He was emphatic. "I'll take care of my son. You just sit tight for a bit." He seemed distracted. "We may have to make a few last-minute maneuvers."

Maneuvers. What in the hell did that mean? My heart went cold. Was it possible that after this conversation, everything could still backfire? Would the Golds still be able to find a way to wrangle the house away from Annie?

"I'll be in my office if you need me then." I tried to keep my voice steady as I stood and excused myself. I turned and left his office and headed down the hallway. I had an uneasy feeling that the situation wasn't yet over, and I had several hours to wait for the other shoe to drop.

Chapter 21

My nerves were on edge for the rest of the day as I contemplated what might be transpiring just down the hall. I had glimpsed Donald Junior as he breezed by my office on his way to his father's, and it was all I could do to sit still and wait to see what would happen.

At three-thirty, Donald's secretary called, summoning me to his office. The look that Millie gave me when I passed her desk made me want to run for cover. I imagined that she could hear every word that was spoken inside those walls.

I knocked on the door and opened it just enough to poke my head inside.

"You wanted to see me, sir?"

"Yes. Come in and shut the door, won't you?"

I did as I was told, closing the door behind me as I entered the office. We were not alone. My client was sitting to one side of the room. His face was beet red, and he didn't meet my eyes.

Warning sirens began going off in my mind. This wasn't a good sign. A confrontation with Donald Junior wasn't exactly what I had in mind.

"Sit down, Kate."

Again, I did as I was told, my eyes darting back and forth between father and son. I began speaking to myself in my mind, trying to calm myself. It wouldn't do to appear nervous at this point.

Donald Senior cleared his throat.

"It appears that we have some work to do." His eyes were on his son, and I began to feel the tension between them.

"I spoke with my son about the information that you've gathered, and it appears that he has no defense." He was addressing me, but his eyes still hadn't left his son.

"Isn't that right, Don?"

The color on the younger man's face darkened as he kept his lips carefully clamped together.

"In fact" — Donald's voice was rising — "my son here has confessed to practically making a living off of stealing from his wife and her store." Again he paused for emphasis. "Isn't that right, Don?" He repeated the question to his son and again received no reply.

For the first time since I entered the room, my

employer turned his gaze to me. "It appears that he's decided to add theft and larceny to his many talents."

I could barely believe what I was hearing. I kept my mouth shut tightly as I returned his stare.

"I insisted that he stay here when I invited you into my office." His smile was forced. "You see, this is just one of many lessons that I've tried over the years to teach him. The point that I am trying to make to him right now is that the humiliation he is suffering at this very moment is nothing" — he paused before raising his voice and turning his attention back to his son — "*nothing* in comparison to the humiliation that you and the members of your family would suffer if your current indiscretions were to be made public."

The contrast between his booming voice and the sudden silence in the room was stark. I realized that I'd been holding my breath and now let it out slowly.

He turned his focus back to me.

"What is the usual prison term for grand larceny?" The question was rhetorical, and he didn't wait for my reply. "Five years? Ten years? Maybe twenty?"

I nodded, knowing that he didn't really expect a response from me. I was merely a prop in his one-person play.

Again the silence was deafening. When he opened his mouth to speak again, his voice was low and threatening.

"Have I made my point, Donald?"

I stole a look at Donald Junior, who was almost cowering in a chair that wasn't big enough to swallow him up. His eyes were averted as he clenched his jaw.

"Donald!"

The younger man jumped to attention. "Yes sir,"

he mumbled as he continued to focus on the carpet in front of his feet.

"Then you are dismissed." Donald's voice was curt. He watched his son stand and head toward the door like a frightened rabbit. I wished I could join him.

Once he'd left the office, I turned my attention back to the man who sat on the other side of the expansive desk. He looked old and tired.

"My apologies for asking you to witness that little tirade of mine." He smiled. "I wanted to make him understand that I meant business." He paused. "I also wanted him to understand the severity of what he did and to suffer some good old-fashioned humiliation. I can only hope that he will learn from this."

I stared at him blankly and dared to ask the question. "Do you think that he will?"

He looked wounded. "I doubt it. But my wife and I are at loose ends with him. He's been a taker his entire life, no matter what his mother and I have tried." His eyes flickered over mine and he almost laughed. "Oh, I know that I'm a real son of a bitch, my dear. But my wife is an absolute angel. She's a kind and generous woman who didn't deserve a son as despicable as what she got." His voice trailed off, and he became preoccupied. Several moments elapsed before he seemed to remember that I was still in the room.

He cleared his throat and composed himself.

"I want you to get hold of Annie's lawyer."

It was the first time that I'd heard her name on Donald's lips.

"I want you to tell him or her that we're willing to drop the fight for the house in Cambridge."

My heart began to flutter, and I found myself tempering my reaction.

"On one condition," he added quickly.

As if he had any grounds for making any demands at all, I thought.

"I want it *in writing* that she will agree not to bring any criminal charges against my son in exchange for us dropping all claims to all joint property." He paused again, scrutinizing my reaction. "Do you think they'll go for that?"

"I can't be certain, sir," I replied. "They have some strong ammunition. But I'll see if I can't persuade them."

"Good." He nodded, satisfied. "Do your best, then. It's getting quite late, and I know you have some calls to make. I won't keep you any longer."

That was that. I had expected the sky to fall around my ears, but instead I was being dismissed to go and do one last piece of dirty work for my employer.

"Let me know as soon as you have an answer." His voice reached my ears as I reached for the doorknob.

I assured him that I would and kept my composure until I'd made it down the hall and into my own office. I shut the door and closed my eyes. "Yes!" I said aloud in a quiet whisper.

I allowed myself a moment of triumph before dropping in the chair behind my desk and reaching for my Rolodex.

Chapter 22

Bob picked up the phone on the very first ring.

"Bob Gleason." He sounded harried.

"Bob, this is Kate Brennan."

"Kate." His voice spoke volumes. "I was hoping to hear from you earlier today."

Panic rose. "I hope I'm not too late."

"That depends, Kate," he replied. "I think you know that."

I felt relief. There was time.

"I think we have an offer that will satisfy everyone, Bob." I tempered my enthusiasm. There were still several hurdles ahead.

"I'm all ears," he said simply.

I paused briefly, making sure that I was about to phrase my words correctly.

"My client is prepared to drop all claims on joint property that he shares with your client. There are a couple of conditions, though."

Bob snorted. "I can't wait to hear this, Kate. It better be good."

I ignored his side comments and continued.

"Mr. Gold would like an agreement in writing stating that your client will not seek to file any criminal charges against him with regard to the misappropriation of funds and merchandise from Treasured Past."

"What?" Confusion filled his voice. "I have no idea what you're talking about, Kate. What's this all about?"

"I think that if you discuss this with your client, she will fill you in on any details that you need to understand." I chose my words carefully, not wanting to say anything that could be misinterpreted or, worse, construed as a breach in Annie's trust. It suddenly became very clear to me that I was making a tremendous leap of faith. I could also lose all my credibility if anyone ever found out that I had used personal information to manipulate my own client. What I had done was completely unethical.

"Kate." Now he sounded aggravated. "This whole thing is a mess that I don't welcome. I don't need any further mysteries here, okay? Tell me what this is about."

I closed my eyes and sighed. Bob wasn't reacting the way I'd expected. He should be filled with enthusiasm that I had managed to find a way for Annie to keep her home.

"Bob, I can't say any more than that." I dropped my voice down to a near whisper. "I'm treading a very thin line, Bob. I think you know that. Just please take this proposal to your client and ask her to fill you in. I honestly believe that she'll be agreeable to the terms."

"This is extremely out of the ordinary, Kate. I have no idea how to advise my client."

"You'll have to ask her for an explanation then, Bob. And as you reminded me, it's getting very late in the day."

Bob groaned. "I'm not happy about this."

His unwillingness was irritating me.

"I understand, Bob. Believe me, you're not the only one."

He ignored my comment and told me not to leave my office. "I want to get this thing squared away tonight. I don't want any more last-minute surprises."

"Fair enough," I told him, then said good-bye to the dial tone in my ear.

Compared to Bob, Melanie was an absolute angel, I decided. Then I made a mental note to let her know how much I appreciated working with her.

I looked at the clock and noted that it was already after four-thirty. I acknowledged the demands for food that my stomach was making and picked up the phone again. It looked like an awfully long evening ahead, and a pizza delivery might just help pass the time.

* * * * *

I tried to imagine Annie's reaction when Bob told her about the offer. She would be confused at first, of that much I was certain. Beyond that, I couldn't be sure. I could never have predicted her behavior over the last week, and I certainly didn't have any idea how she might react to this new twist. She would probably be angry with me for disclosing what I'd learned about Donald's stealing from her store. She also probably wouldn't trust that the offer was completely aboveboard. She would be suspicious, at least. But hopefully, once she explained to Bob what it was all about, he would be able to counsel her to take the offer.

At six-thirty, Donald Gold stuck his head in my office.

"Have you heard anything yet?"

I had been staring off into space, fantasizing that Annie would be so happy and excited about the turn of events that she would be waiting on my doorstep when I finally made it home.

"No. Not yet." It took a moment to gather my thoughts and focus on Donald.

He nodded grimly. "I'll be in my office. Let me know when you hear anything."

"I will, sir," I promised, and was thankful when he disappeared back into the hallway. I didn't think I could take the waiting much longer.

At seven forty-five, my phone finally rang and I lunged for it. "Kate Brennan."

"Kate? Bob Gleason." He cut out all the formalities. "We have a counteroffer."

My stomach dropped. Any hope and patience that I'd had earlier in the day had vanished.

"Let's have it." I was all business too.

Bob suddenly seemed to be enjoying this far too much.

"My client has agreed to your offer in principle, with one small caveat."

I rolled my eyes. What the hell was Annie up to now?

"And that would be . . ." I was tapping my pen as I held the phone to my ear.

"She is seeking some financial compensation."

My heart sank. *Oh no, Annie. You're going too far. Now you're going to ask for money too?*

"How much?" I squeezed my eyelids together and gritted my teeth.

Bob paused far too long before speaking.

"She would like reimbursement for all losses that the store has incurred as a result of your client's actions.

That's it? That's all? Now I was grinning.

"And do you have a number for that, Bob?"

"Not yet, I'm afraid. We would like thirty days to perform a complete audit before coming up with a final number."

My smile was full. "That certainly sounds fair enough to me, as long as we can get it all in writing." I paused, wanting desperately to ask Bob about Annie's reaction. But I couldn't. "Let me go right now and present this to my client. Can I reach you in your office in about fifteen minutes?"

He told me that he was on his way home and gave me his cell phone number.

"Thanks for your help, Bob. I'm sure we'll be able to get this squared away tonight."

"Let's hope so. And Kate?"

"Yes?" I was in a hurry to hang up the phone and present the offer to Donald.

"Bravo." He practically whispered the word before hanging up the phone. I stared at the receiver for several moments and allowed the moment to wash over me. Then I placed it back in its cradle and took one more deep breath. We were in the homestretch now.

Donald was staring out his window when I entered his office.

"Excuse me, sir?'

"Yes, dear." His eyes were tired when they met mine.

"They've accepted the offer with one condition, sir."

He raised a single brow in reply.

"She would like to be reimbursed for the money that your son —" I found myself searching for the right word, not wanting to offend him.

"Stole from her?" He finished the sentence for me. "That seems more than reasonable, I suppose. How much are we talking about?"

"They're not certain. They'd like thirty days to complete an audit."

He nodded, digesting the news. Then his eyes lifted to mine. "It's odd that they wouldn't have an exact figure, though, don't you think? Considering that the court date is tomorrow and I would have expected them to spring all of this on us then."

I was frozen in my tracks. Had I dropped my guard? Is this the moment when Donald would drop the bomb on me?

He regarded me closely as I mustered my courage.

"It's my understanding that your son's wife just changed representation last week. Perhaps that has something to do with it." I stared at him boldly, willing him to call my bluff.

"Hm," was his only reaction. "Her first lawyer probably wasn't doing the job," he surmised. "Sounds like the replacement is on the ball."

He took several steps forward and picked up his suit jacket from where it lay on one chair. "Very well. I've drafted an agreement that we can modify in the morning." He reached over to his desk and picked up a piece of paper that he held out to me. "I'd like a signature before the case gets finalized at two. Can you arrange that?"

I nodded. "I will, Donald." My eyes did a cursory glance at the agreement.

He was ushering me from his office.

"Thank you, Kate. Again, I appreciate your loyalty and discretion in this matter." He made an attempt at a smile as he passed me in the hallway. "See you in the morning."

"Good night, sir."

His sigh was heavy. "Let's hope so, Kate. I've got to tell my wife about everything that happened today."

"I'm sorry, sir." I did feel sympathy.

His only reply was a raised hand as he sauntered toward the elevators.

I wasted no time in contacting Bob to tell him the good news. We arranged to meet in the courthouse at one o'clock the next afternoon. Plenty of time to exchange signatures and papers before the divorce was made final by the courts.

* * * * *

Everything went according to plan. Bob was all smiles as he shook my hand and handed me a signed copy of the agreement that I'd faxed earlier in the day.

I had foolishly hoped that Annie would be there to sign the document before me, and I tried to hide my disappointment at her absence.

Our time in front of the judge was brief as we agreed to the settlement as outlined in the agreement. Within ten minutes the divorce was final. And Annie still had her house.

"Well done, Counselor." Bob patted my shoulder as he smiled. "I'm not quite sure that I understand all of the details —"

"It's probably best that way," I told him.

He laughed. "Probably. I'm just glad that things turned out well for Annie. She's a really fine lady, Kate."

I wasn't sure how much he knew about our relationship, so I decided to play it safe.

"How was she when you spoke with her, Bob? I hope she was pleased."

He laughed. "She was bug-eyed furious at first. It took awhile to calm her down. She was convinced that this was just another ploy on their part. But once we got a copy of the agreement this morning I was able to convince her that everything was on the up and up."

I wasn't surprised by his description of her reaction. I only hoped that she was satisfied with the settlement.

"I'm just glad it's over," I told him awkwardly. I was suddenly very sad, wondering if I'd ever get the chance to talk to Annie again and try to figure out if we could put all of this behind us.

"Ask her to call me sometime, will you?" I realized that my throat was tightening as I spoke the words.

His expression was somewhat bewildered. "I'll do that, Kate." He held out his hand, and I took it in mine. "Take care."

"Thanks. You too." I mustered a small smile before turning and heading outside the courthouse. It was an abnormally hot and humid August day. I should have been full of joy, but instead all I could think about was Annie.

My shoulders felt heavy with the weight of the world. *We should be celebrating right now,* I thought. But she'd made it quite clear the last time we spoke that she didn't want me in her life. I wouldn't reach out to her. Not again.

Chapter 23

The great room was finally finished. Cherry bookcases lined one wall from floor to ceiling. Tung oil had been rubbed into the rich wood, bringing it alive and showing off its natural grain and beauty.

The window had been installed and was complete as well. Even the stone chimney had been scrubbed clean of the white paint until each stone winked and gleamed in the sunlight. The fireplace begged for a fire to be built and enjoyed. But I found no pleasure in the completion of the project. For me, it marked the end of my very short love affair with Annie. And so the fireplace stayed cold, and the room remained empty.

Both Beth and Melanie had come to my rescue in the weeks that followed the end of Annie's divorce case. They both did their best to help me to forget about Annie and move on with my life.

"You should consider coming back to family law, Kate. You can't possibly be happy working at that place anymore." Melanie picked up a carrot and placed it in her mouth, crunching loudly. She and Beth were at my house, where we'd spent the day barbequing and lounging and doing next to nothing.

"Oh, Mel. I don't know." The thought of changing jobs after everything that had happened over the past months exhausted me.

Melanie and Beth shared a knowing look between them.

"What?" I asked the question of them both, my eyes floating back and forth between them.

"She's right, Kate," Beth chirped in. "You hate it there."

I picked through my salad until I found a tomato. I popped it in my mouth and chewed slowly. The last thing I wanted to discuss right then was my job.

"You're both right," I told them. "I hate working there. I hate the fact that they're bilking clients left and right and squashing all the little guys." I picked up a stick of celery and heard its satisfying crunch as it reached my mouth.

They were both staring at me, waiting for me to swallow.

"So?" Mel asked.

"I'm not ready to make a change, Melanie. The thought alone exhausts me." The looks on their faces told me that they weren't convinced. "Besides, I don't know what I would do."

"That's easy. Come back to the center."

I glared hard in Melanie's direction. "We've had this conversation before, Mel. You know why I left and why I won't go back."

"Kate." Beth was leaning forward now, eyes gentle as searched my eyes. "You have to stop blaming yourself for my losing custody of Billy. It wasn't your fault, and things have turned out pretty well for us since then."

Beth and I had never discussed how I felt about losing her case. Even when I'd abruptly changed jobs, I never talked to her about my reasons.

It was all I could do to look at her.

"You trusted me to help you with the most important thing in your life, and I failed," I told her. "How can I let that go? How can I just pretend it never happened?"

"Because you have to," was her reply. "I've never blamed you for what happened. I've never thought for one moment that you didn't do everything in your power to get custody of Billy." She reached across the table and held my hand.

"You didn't fail us, Kate. The system did. The puritanical judge that sat on that bench didn't listen to a word you said. The only thing that mattered to him was that I'm a lesbian. He had his mind made up before the case even started."

Melanie was leaning forward now too. "It's true, Kate, and you know it. Just think about it. How can you just walk away from the injustices of our judicial system? How can you turn your back when you know that what it really needs is someone to fight back?

Someone who is willing to represent all those people who otherwise wouldn't stand a chance without your help? Just think about the number of lives you've touched and made better."

"I think they would have done just fine without me." I lifted a bottle of beer to my lips.

Beth released my hand. "That's ridiculous, and you know it. Do you want me to list all of the people you've helped over the years just to refresh your memory?"

I was feeling cornered and chastised.

"And don't tell me that you're sick of it, either," Melanie chimed in. "I've never seen you more spirited than when you're taking on a particular lawsuit or client. It's in your blood."

I stared from one to the other.

"Are you both forgetting that I didn't have a life back then? Do you remember the hours I used to spend at the office? I rarely even saw the inside of my house."

Beth was quick to reply. "Forgive me, Kate. You can blame your profession for your lack of personal life if you want to. But the fact is that you really just need to find some balance. There's nothing wrong with putting in a few extra hours here and there, but you have to know when to walk away."

They were both right, of course. But I wasn't ready to give in so easily.

"Did you just say that I have no personal life?" I narrowed my eyes to tease her.

"Well, yeah. I suppose. At least you didn't before you met Annie."

Ouch. Her name was like a knife in my heart. I

must have reacted to the mention of her name, because Beth was quick to apologize.

"I'm sorry, Kate. I wasn't thinking."

I waved her worry aside. "It's okay. I'm going to have to get used to hearing her name sooner or later."

"Have you heard from her?" Melanie joined the conversation again.

I shook my head. "What about you?"

She nodded slowly. "She called earlier this week. She apologized for the way that she fired me. She admitted that she'd been unreasonable and thanked me for everything I had done."

I was suddenly envious. So Annie had reached out to Mel. At least that meant that she was finally beginning to relax and think rationally.

"That's good, I suppose," Beth said. "Don't you think?" She turned back to me.

I nodded.

Melanie hesitated a moment before speaking again. "I also mentioned to her that it was really you that she should be thanking. I told her that you really jeopardized your professional integrity and reputation by pulling off what you did." She glanced over at Beth. "Can you even imagine what would have happened if Gold had known all along that the two of them were seeing each other?"

Beth grimaced. "It would have been a disaster."

We were silent while my thoughts turned back to Annie.

"It sounds like she's doing well then," I said aloud. My words met with blank stares. "I'm glad she's okay."

* * * * *

Life began to change rather quickly from there. Within another week, Donald was in my office with a big smile on his face.

"I just wanted to let you know that everything's been finalized. I had a check sent to Annie this morning, so everything should be squared away now."

I had no idea what he expected for a response, or why he had bothered to come in and tell me about it. My interaction with the senior partner had been limited in recent weeks to brief hellos in the hallway.

"I'm glad to hear it," was my lame reply.

"Now that everything has settled down, I just wanted to come by and thank you again for everything you did. My wife and I appreciate the fact that you were able to circumvent a disaster before it blew up in our faces." I'd rarely heard such a long monolog from his lips.

"It was my pleasure, sir." What else could I say?

"No, dear. I don't think that it was." He seemed to search his brain to come up with the right words. "I think that I underestimated both you and your abilities. I treated you poorly, and I'd like to make up for that."

He lifted one hand and reached into his breast pocket. He removed a long thin white envelope and placed in on my desk in front of me.

I stared at the envelope, and then at him.

"Open it," he insisted, and I complied. Inside the envelope was a check for twenty thousand dollars. I counted the zeros twice before raising my eyes back to his.

"I can't accept this, Donald." I placed the check back in the envelope and pushed it to the end of the desk.

"It's just a small thank-you. A bonus, if you like."

"I appreciate your generosity, Donald. But I can't take the money." It was bad enough that I had essentially lied and manipulated him into dropping the petition against Annie. It was another thing entirely to take his money for doing it. I may have been pleased that I was able to make sure that Annie kept her house, but I still continued to deal with some guilt.

Donald appeared stunned. I supposed that no one had ever turned down his money before.

"But why not, Kate? You did a fine job for me, and I promised to make it worth your while. And believe me, the pain and suffering that you saved my family is worth many times the amount of that check."

I didn't want to offend him, but I was resolute.

"As I said, Donald, I appreciate it. But I can't accept it."

"Don't be ridiculous." He was growing angry.

"Donald" — I interrupted him — "I can't accept it because I'm leaving the firm."

I don't know which one of us was more surprised. I'd certainly been thinking about the possibility, but I hadn't known I'd made the decision.

He no longer appeared surprised. Instead, he accepted my declaration with a nod of his head.

"You're not cut out for corporate law, are you." It was a statement, not a question. Obviously he had noticed my lack of enthusiasm.

I wrinkled my nose. "I'm afraid my heart's just not in it, sir."

He nodded. For a moment it occurred to me that I should be mad that he wasn't trying to talk me out of it. But apparently I hadn't been fooling anyone.

"When will you be leaving?"

I honestly didn't know. Now that I'd committed to leaving, I guess I had some decisions to make.

"I'm not quite sure. There are a number of decisions that I have to make. I have to find another firm that's willing to take me on." I laughed and watched him smile.

"Then why don't you accept this check as your severance package," he suggested. "Clean up a few things here and turn your cases over to Barbara. Then you can take some time to decide what you really want to do."

I returned his gaze for a few moments, ready to protest.

"I won't take no for an answer, Kate. Take the check as our thanks." He turned to head for the door. "Best of luck to you, Kate."

"Thanks," I muttered, but he was already gone.

I suppose it was inevitable that I would rejoin Melanie at the Cambridge Family Law Center. Within weeks I had leased space in the building and had begun the task of moving my law books and necessities into my office.

There was the small task of having to buy office furniture, and it was Beth who made the obvious observation.

"Gee, too bad you didn't know you were going to be moving before we took all your old office furniture to Treasured Past."

I grimaced at the memory.

"Did she ever sell it?" Beth asked.

"I have no idea. It hadn't sold the last time I was there." My eyes floated over Beth. "Don't go getting any ideas, sweetie. If you think I'm going over there to retrieve that furniture, you're out of your mind."

Beth shrugged. "I'll go."

"No you won't." I was adamant.

"Why not? It makes perfect sense." She was matter-of-fact.

"You will not go over there for me, Beth."

"Ooh." She glared at me. "Are you telling me what I can and cannot do?"

"When it comes to this, yes, I am."

She slid me a mischievous look. "Don't push my buttons, Kate. You're giving me ideas."

"Well, don't. Please." I faked a smile. "Besides, I'm really thinking about going with something a lot more modern. Something kind of light and less imposing."

Beth didn't believe me. "That doesn't sound like you."

"It's what I want," I snapped. "Do you want to go shopping for office furniture with me?"

Beth laughed. "You sure know how to have a good time." She complained for a while longer before we got in my car and began the search.

After three days, Beth made it clear that she'd had enough. "You hate everything you look at and you're driving me crazy. Why don't you just start looking at some antiques? You'll be much happier."

"And you will be too?" I teased.

"Exactly."

I considered her suggestion. "I don't think I have it in me. It could take weeks to find something that I like."

Beth groaned. "There is one other possibility."

"Don't even say it, Beth."

She was annoyed. "Then you're on your own, sweetie. I've had enough." She left me sulking on my front porch steps.

Fine, I decided, I'd begin searching antique stores in the morning. Except that tomorrow was Sunday. Fine, I'll start on Monday. What I wouldn't do, though, was start going to auctions. I wanted to make sure there was no chance of running into Annie.

On Sunday evening I received a call from Melanie, asking if I could meet her the following morning. "I'm running into some trouble on a case that I'm working on, and I think you might be able to help me."

"But I'm not officially there yet," I told her.

"Only because you don't have any flipping furniture," she retorted. "No excuse. I need your help."

"Okay, okay. I'll be there." *Damn.* Why was everyone getting so upset about this furniture thing?

There was a box of office supplies that had been sitting beside my front door for weeks. As I left the next morning, I remembered to pick it up and bring it along. Time to stop screwing around, I decided. I'd have to pick up some furniture that week.

Melanie wasn't in her office when I arrived, so I tucked my box of supplies under one arm and headed down the hall to my office. Sliding the key in the lock, I turned the knob and pushed open the door.

I stopped in my tracks, staring into the room. My old mahogany desk stood in the center. The matching credenza stood behind it, and the bookcase was against one wall. My emotions ran from wanting to cry to wanting to kill someone.

178

"Looks good, doesn't it?" Melanie sneaked up behind me.

"Perfect," I admitted, stepping into the room and setting the box down on the floor. I let my fingers run across the smooth surface of the desk and felt my heart ache. Annie had to have been involved in this. At least partially.

"So is this your doing?" I asked Mel.

"Only partially," she admitted. "It's mostly Beth's fault. She did the dirty work and went to pick it up. I met her here and helped her unload it."

I searched her eyes and she knew what I was thinking.

"No. Annie isn't here."

My lips clamped together, and I nodded. Standing back to take another look around, I was more than satisfied.

"It really looks great, Mel. Thank you."

"You should thank Beth," she told me.

I laughed. "I may throttle her instead. I told her not to do this."

"I know. But it really did make sense."

I couldn't argue. Besides, it really did seem perfect.

"Why don't we take a look at this case that you dragged me down here for. How can I help?"

"I lied," she grinned. "I just wanted to get you here before you had a chance to pick up something else."

I laughed. "You're so devious," I teased. "What are you doing now? Want to help me unpack?"

"Ooh. Physical labor? Are you kidding?" She started backing away. "I don't think so, Kate. You're on your own."

Without another word, she disappeared from my office and left me alone to stand and look around, taking it all in. Eagerness settled over me, and I began opening boxes, emptying their contents everywhere, and finding the perfect spot for each and every item.

Chapter 24

Something felt strange the moment that I walked into my house. I walked into the living room and stopped to look around and listen. Nothing seemed out of place, and the house was silent. But the goose bumps rising on my arms told me that something wasn't right.

Had someone been here? I glanced out the front window but saw nothing out of the ordinary except for the older model Volvo wagon parked in front of my house. I'd never seen the car before, and the sight of it only managed to cause more shivers to slide along my spine. Something was definitely not right.

I set my car keys down on the coffee table and went to the kitchen, but found nothing out of place. Returning to the living room, I saw that the pocket doors to the great room were cracked open by a few inches. My skin began to crawl.

Cautiously, I inched my way to the doorway and peered through one of the panes of glass.

I held my breath. Annie was sitting on the window seat, only her profile visible as she stared out through the glass. I was frozen in place, my eyes taking in a vision that I didn't think I would ever see again. She was wearing one of the sundresses that I'd grown so fond of, her hair tied back in a single braid.

If she knew that I was watching her, she gave no indication. She looked calm and peaceful, oblivious of my watching eyes.

Taking a deep breath, I reached for the handle to the door and slid it open. I waited for her to look my way, but she continued to gaze out the window, her eyes steady.

It was apparent that I would have to make the first move, so I stepped cautiously into the room.

"It's quite lovely." Her voice reached my ears when I was several feet away from her, and I stopped.

I didn't reply, and her focus finally fell on me. "The room, I mean. It turned out just as we'd envisioned it."

The sight of her almost took my breath away. I didn't know how to respond or why she was here. My instinct was sarcasm. Probably not the best choice.

"You mean the way *you* envisioned it."

I watched her blink twice before she spoke.

"It could use some furniture, though. Don't you think?"

I was surprised to find that it was anger that began to boil in my veins. Who did she think she was? She had accused me of the vilest behavior and tossed me from her life. Now she just shows up on my doorstep and wants to talk about *decorating*?

"You know that decorating and remodeling aren't exactly my strong suit." I tried to keep the sarcasm from my voice.

Her lips curled up on one side.

"I'm sorry. That's not quite the way I wanted to start this conversation." She averted her eyes momentarily as I kept silent.

"I wanted to talk to you," she began.

"You couldn't just pick up the phone?"

Her eyes were steady now. "I didn't think you'd talk to me, if you want the truth."

Would I have talked to her? I couldn't imagine that I wouldn't have.

"So you decided just to show up?" My voice sounded stern and distant, the opposite of what I was feeling.

"Actually, it was Beth who convinced me —"

"Beth put you up to this?" I was incredulous.

"No, no." She lifted a hand in my direction. "Don't be mad at Beth. I've wanted to talk to you for some time. When she came to the store yesterday I asked about you. She convinced me that you don't hate me and that I should come over."

I held back my smile.

"Do you hate me, Kate?" She was smiling nervously.

"Of course not, Annie. How could I?" My knees felt weak, and I covered the few feet between us and joined her on the window seat. I sat several feet away, watching as she stared down at the floor at nothing in particular.

"I should have come and talked to you weeks ago," she began. Her voice was steady but she kept her eyes from mine. "But I was just so ashamed of myself."

I didn't know what to say and so I was silent, allowing her to continue.

"I said some ugly things to you. I accused you of plotting and planning against me. I can't believe I ever could have thought those things."

"Did you honestly think that I would have intentionally set out to hurt you that way?" As much as I wanted to make things easy for her, I needed some answers.

"I don't think that I was thinking at all," she told me. "All I heard was Donald's name, and suddenly I didn't trust anything or anyone." She raised her eyes to mine. "I know it's no excuse, but you have no idea how miserable that man and his family have made my life. All I could think of was that they had found yet another way to destroy me." She was shaking her head. "I was completely irrational, Kate. I should have listened to you and believed in you. I'm sorry."

I was finally hearing her words that I had dreamt she would say. But something still unsettled me.

"Why did you lie to me, Annie? Why did you tell me you were divorced?"

Her sigh was heavy as her eyes dropped back to

184

the floor. "There were a number of reasons. But none of them make much sense now," she admitted.

"At first I didn't tell you because I thought that you might be completely put off by the fact that you were seeing a married woman. The divorce was supposed to be final in a couple of months, and I reasoned that it was only a little lie."

The excuse sounded lame.

"The other reason that I didn't tell you, and the reason that I was careful about keeping you away from the house, was because I was constantly afraid that Donald would somehow find out about the two of us. He had already made such an ugly scene when he found out that I was with another woman. The last thing that I wanted was to give him more ammunition before the case was final."

I believed what she was saying, but it still seemed to me that she'd gone to extreme lengths to keep her life a secret from me.

"I can't believe that you didn't tell me that all these things were going on with you. Annie, I could have helped you."

"I know that now. But at the time I didn't trust that you wouldn't walk away if you knew how complicated things were."

I shook my head. "You didn't trust me."

"No," she admitted. "I probably didn't. It was difficult for me to believe that you actually cared enough to help me through it."

"That's ridiculous, Annie." None of it made sense.

"Maybe to you it does. But after years and years of living with that man, I learned the hard way not to trust anyone."

I was listening to her words, trying to understand and even sympathize. But I felt empty.

"So what made you come here today?" I asked quietly.

Another loud sigh. "To apologize. And to thank you for what you did." She was fidgeting, trying to smile. "Bob told me what little he knew. Melanie filled me in on the rest. You took a big risk, Kate."

I shrugged. "Probably. The truth is that I hated Gold even before I knew he was your husband. I tried to come up with all kinds of ideas to keep him from getting the house. Then when I found out it was you . . ." I shivered at the memory.

We sat together awkwardly for a full minute while I fidgeted, trying to find something to do with my hands. The silence was finally broken when Annie stood abruptly.

"I guess I should go."

She caught me so off guard that I simply stared at her. She must have taken my lack of reply as an acknowledgment of some kind, because she gave me a curt nod and began walking toward the door.

Anger flooded through me. "Wait a minute," I called out, jumping to my feet. She stopped cold and turned to face me.

The expression in her eyes hovered between fear and sadness.

"That's it?" I demanded. "I don't hear from you in nearly two months and you just show up here and clear your conscience and then walk away?" I was furious.

She continued to stare at me, remaining speechless.

"No 'Gee, Kate, how have you been?' or 'Hi, Kate, what have you been doing lately?' "

She looked so sad and all I wanted to do was shake her or kiss her or make her laugh. Anything to put a smile on that beautiful face.

My voice softened as my heart began to weaken. "How about 'It's good to see you, Kate. I've missed you.' "

A slow smile found her lips. She cleared her throat and took a deep breath. "Hi, Kate. It's good to see you," she repeated my words until her smile reached her eyes. "I've missed you." She paused. "Very much."

I forgot about the accusations and mistrust.

"I've missed you too," I told her.

"Do you think you can ever forgive me?" I thought that I could see a glimmer of tears in her eyes.

"Do you think you can ever trust me?"

Her smile became lopsided. "Touche."

Again we stood awkwardly, the fight now gone completely.

"Are you seeing anyone, Counselor?"

I laughed. "You know better than that, Annie."

"Just fishing." She grinned, and I nodded. It was so good just to see her face, to hear her voice.

"Why, did you have someone in mind?" I asked coyly.

She nodded. "I did, actually. I was thinking somewhere along the lines of a reconciliation."

Now I was smiling. "With you?"

She grew suddenly shy. "If you'll have me."

"You know that I will," I told her. "But I think you know that we have an awful lot of talking to do."

"That we do, Kate." She took slow steps to cover

the distance between us. "And I promise that I'll tell you every boring and gruesome detail of my life, if you still want me to."

"I do. Every detail."

She was so close now that I could have reached out and touched her. I could smell her freshness and see the small creases around her eyes.

"But before I start, I was thinking that what I'd really like, more that anything, is just to hold you."

My heart was beating loudly as I lifted my arms. We settled into each other, wrapping arms around one another and holding on for the longest time.

"Oh, Kate," she murmured against my ear. "I can't believe how foolish I was." I could tell by the sound of her voice that she was crying.

"It's okay, Annie. We'll work everything out." There was nothing I wanted more.

"I still want to grow old with you, you know." Her lips were still pressed against my ear, but she seemed calmer now.

"Is that a proposal?" I smiled, remembering the conversation we'd had many weeks ago.

"Yes," she replied without hesitation.

I lifted my head to stare into her eyes. "Wait a minute," I laughed. "I thought you had some rule about not getting married until you knew someone for at least a year."

She laughed too, eyes glistening. "Honey, after everything that's happened in the last few months, I'm not taking anything for granted." She leaned forward until her forehead was pressed to mine. "I'm so sorry that I hurt you, Kate. I love you so much."

Had I heard her correctly? I searched her eyes and

saw the mixture of emotions that left no doubt about how she felt.

I touched her lips with mine. "I love you too, Annie." Our lips came together, lightly at first, remembering. I shivered in her arms, basking in the moment. Then our kiss became urgent and demanding. We had two very long months of separation to make up for.

About the Author

Originally born and raised in Iowa, Linda now splits her time between her home in Massachusetts and her new gal, Bella, in Florida. While her biggest complaint remains that there simply aren't enough hours in the day to do everything she'd like, she still insists that she's the luckiest woman alive. Maggie continues to be the sweetest thing that Linda has ever known.

IN EVERY PORT by Karin Kallmaker. 224 pp. Jessica's sexy, adventuresome travels.
ISBN 1-931513-36-8 $12.95

TOUCHWOOD by Karin Kallmaker. 240 pp. Loving May/December romance.
ISBN 1-931513-37-6 $12.95

WATERMARK by Karin Kallmaker. 248 pp. One burning question . . . how to lead her back to love?
ISBN 1-931513-38-4 $12.95

EMBRACE IN MOTION by Karin Kallmaker. 240 pp. A whirlwind love affair.
ISBN 1-931513-39-2 $12.95

ONE DEGREE OF SEPARATION by Karin Kallmaker. 232 pp. Can an Iowa City librarian find love and passion when a California girl surfs into the close-knit dyke capital of the Midwest?
ISBN 1-931513-30-9 $12.95

CRY HAVOC A Detective Franco Mystery by Baxter Clare. 240 pp. A dead hustler with a headless rooster in his lap sends Lt. L.A. Franco headfirst against Mother Love.
ISBN 1-931513931-7 $12.95

DISTANT THUNDER by Peggy J. Herring. 294 pp. Bankrobbing drifter Cordy awakens strange new feelings in Leo in this romantic tale set in the Old West.
ISBN 1-931513-28-7 $12.95

COP OUT by Claire McNab. 216 pp. 4th Detective Inspector Carol Ashton Mystery.
ISBN 1-931513-29-5 $12.95

BLOOD LINK by Claire McNab. 159 pp. 15th Detective Inspector Carol Ashton Mystery. Is Carol unwittingly playing into a deadly plan?
ISBN 1-931513-27-9 $12.95

TALK OF THE TOWN by Saxon Bennett. 239 pp. With enough beer, barbecue and B.S., anything is possible!
ISBN 1-931513-18-X $12.95

MAYBE NEXT TIME by Karin Kallmaker. 256 pp. Sabrina Starling has it all: fame, money, women—and pain. Nothing hurts like the one that got away. ISBN 1-931513-26-0 $12.95

WHEN GOOD GIRLS GO BAD: A Motor City Thriller by Therese Szymanski. 230 pp. Brett, Randi, and Allie join forces to stop a serial killer. ISBN 1-931513-11-2 $12.95

A DAY TOO LONG: A Helen Black Mystery by Pat Welch. 328 pp. This time Helen's fate is in her own hands.
ISBN 1-931513-22-8 $12.95

THE RED LINE OF YARMALD by Diana Rivers. 256 pp. The Hadra's only hope lies in a magical red line . . . climactic sequel to *Clouds of War*. ISBN 1-931513-23-6 $12.95

OUTSIDE THE FLOCK by Jackie Calhoun. 224 pp. Jo embraces her new love and life.
ISBN 1-931513-13-9 $12.95

LEGACY OF LOVE by Marianne K. Martin. 224 pp. Read the whole Sage Bristo story.
ISBN 1-931513-15-5 $12.95

STREET RULES: A Detective Franco Mystery by Baxter Clare. 304 pp. Gritty, fast-paced mystery with compelling Detective L.A. Franco ISBN 1-931513-14-7 $12.95

RECOGNITION FACTOR: 4th Denise Cleever Thriller by Claire McNab. 176 pp. Denise Cleever tracks a notorious terrorist to America. ISBN 1-931513-24-4 $12.95

NORA AND LIZ by Nancy Garden. 296 pp. Lesbian romance by the author of *Annie on My Mind*.
ISBN 1931513-20-1 $12.95

MIDAS TOUCH by Frankie J. Jones. 208 pp. Sandra had everything but love.
ISBN 1-931513-21-X $12.95